CHILDREN OF EXILE

**CHILDREN OF EXILE:
VOLUME 1**

CHILDREN
OF EXILE

MARGARET PETERSON
HADDIX

SIMON & SCHUSTER BOOKS FOR YOUNG READERS

NEW YORK LONDON TORONTO SYDNEY NEW DELHI

SIMON & SCHUSTER BOOKS FOR YOUNG READERS

An imprint of Simon & Schuster Children's Publishing Division

1230 Avenue of the Americas, New York, New York 10020

SIMON & SCHUSTER BOOKS FOR YOUNG READERS is a trademark of Simon & Schuster, Inc.

For information about special discounts for bulk purchases, please contact Simon & Schuster Special Sales at 1-866-506-1949 or business@simonandschuster.com.

The Simon & Schuster Speakers Bureau can bring authors to your live event. For more information or to book an event, contact the Simon & Schuster Speakers Bureau at 1-866-248-3049 or visit our website at www.simonspeakers.com.

Jacket design by Krista Vossen

Interior design by Tom Daly

The text for this book is set in Weiss Std

Manufactured in the United States of America

0816 FFG

First Edition

2 4 6 8 10 9 7 5 3 1

Library of Congress Cataloging-in-Publication Data

Names: Haddix, Margaret Peterson, author.

Title: Children of exile / Margaret Peterson Haddix.

Description: New York : Simon & Schuster Books for Young Readers, [2016] |

Summary: A twelve-year-old girl raised in a foster village is returned to her biological parents, and discovers home is not what she expected it to be.

Identifiers: LCCN 2015031239| ISBN 9781442450035 (hardcover) | ISBN 9781442450059 (eBook)

Subjects: | CYAC: Parent and child—Fiction. | Science fiction.

Classification: LCC PZ7.H1164 Ch 2016 | DDC [Fic]—dc23

LC record available at http://lccn.loc.gov/2015031239

For the kids of Montaña de Luz

CHAPTER ONE

We weren't orphans after all.

That was the first surprise.

The second was that we were going home.

"Home!" my little brother, Bobo, sang as he jumped up and down on my bed, right after the Freds told us the news. "Home, home, home, home . . ."

I grabbed him mid-jump and teased, "Silly, you've never even been there before! How do you know it's worth jumping on the bed for?"

"I was born there, right?" Bobo said. "So I do know, Rosi. I *remember*."

He blinked up at me, his long, dark eyelashes sweeping his cheeks like a pair of exquisite feathers. Bobo was five; he had curls that sprang out from his head like so many exclamation points, and his big eyes always seemed to glow. If he'd known how adorable he was, he would have been dangerous.

But there was a rule in Fredtown that you couldn't tell little kids how cute they were.

It was kind of hard to obey.

"How could you remember being such a tiny baby?" I asked. "You were only a few days old when you arrived in Fredtown. *None* of us were more than a few days old, coming here."

I tried to keep my voice light and teasing. I was twelve; I should have known better than to look to a five-year-old to answer my questions.

But no one else had given me the answers I wanted. And sometimes Bobo heard things.

"Edwy says home is where we belong," Bobo said, stubbornly sticking out his lower lip. "Edwy says we should have stayed there always."

"Oh, *Edwy* says," I teased. But it was hard to keep the edge out of my voice.

Of course Edwy has an answer, I thought. *Even if he just made it up. Even if he knows it's a lie.*

Edwy was twelve, like me—we were the oldest children in Fredtown. We were born on the same day. And we were the only ones who were moved to Fredtown on the very day of our birth, instead of waiting a day or two like everyone else. The Freds always told us it had been too "dangerous" for us to stay with our parents then. For the past twelve years, they'd said it was too "dangerous" for any of us children to go home.

I was maybe three the first time I asked, *But isn't it dangerous for our parents, too? Why didn't they come to Fredtown to be safe with us?*

The Freds always said, *They are adults. You are children. Adults have to take care of themselves. It is our job to take care of you.*

I didn't think that counted as a real answer.

That was why Edwy and I had decided when we were ten—back when we still talked to each other—that we were probably orphans and the Freds just didn't want to make us sad by telling us that.

We'd argued about this a little: I said surely the newest babies of Fredtown weren't orphans. Surely *their* parents were still alive.

"But there haven't been any new babies in my family since me," Edwy said fiercely. He always got fierce when the only other choice was sounding sad. "And none in yours since Bobo."

Once he said that, I could see lots of other evidence. If our parents were still alive, wouldn't they at least send us a letter every now and then? Wouldn't they have done everything they possibly could to come get us?

Didn't they know where we were?

When I asked the Freds questions like that, they patted me on the head and told me I was too young to understand.

3

Or they talked about how life was made up of hard choices and, as our guardians, they had chosen what was best for all of us children. And what was best for civilization itself.

The way the Freds talked was tricky. You had to wrap your mind around their words sometimes and turn them inside out to try to figure out what they were really saying.

The way Edwy talked was tricky, too.

"Rosi!" Bobo said, squirming against my grip. "I want to jump some more!"

If any of the Freds saw us, I would be in trouble. I was twelve and Bobo was five; it was wrong for someone who was bigger and older and stronger to overpower someone smaller and younger and weaker. It was wrong to hold someone who didn't want to be held.

"Fine," I told Bobo. "But mess up your own bed, not mine."

I turned and deposited him on his own cot. I was tempted to tickle him too, to try to bring back his glee and his ear-to-ear grin. But that would have required my asking him first, *Is it all right if I tickle you?* And I didn't have the patience for that just then.

Bobo didn't spring instantly to his feet like I expected. He didn't go back to bouncing. He just sat in a heap on his own bed and asked, as if he'd just now thought of the question: "Rosi, *is* it safe to go home now? Why was it too dangerous before but safe now?"

I ruffled his hair and made my voice as light and carefree as a summer breeze.

"You know things can change, you little apple dumpling, you," I said, using the baby name our Fred-parents had given Bobo years ago. "You know the Freds wouldn't send us home if it wasn't safe."

I wasn't like Edwy. I didn't usually lie. Not on purpose.

So why did I feel like I was lying to Bobo now?

CHAPTER TWO

Fredtown was a simple place. If I thought way back to when I was really little, I could remember when only a handful of families lived here, in only a small cluster of buildings. Even now, there were only sixteen blocks of houses, each block a perfect square laid out in grids as precise as the graph paper Edwy and I used for geometry homework. The school, the park, the library, the town hall, and the marketplace stood in the center of the town, surrounded by all the houses.

These were the kinds of questions the little kids asked when the Freds first told us we were going home:

Can we take the park with us?

Can we take our houses?

Can we take our toys?

Who will play in the park if we're not here? Won't the playground and our houses and our toys miss us?

When they gathered us all together to tell us we were

going home, the Freds seemed to want to answer *only* the little kids' questions. When Edwy or I—or any of the almost-as-old-as-us kids—raised our hands, the Freds caught our eyes and shook their heads subtly, the way they always did when they wanted to say, *Not in front of the little ones. We'll talk about your questions later.*

Later hadn't come yet.

Instead, the Fred-parents were meeting at the town hall, so all of us older kids were looking after the little girls and boys.

I was just lucky Bobo was the only little one I was in charge of today. I was lucky I hadn't been given responsibility for the ones who didn't have a brother or sister old enough to babysit, like the Calim sisters (ages four, three, two, and one) or Peki and Meki, the toddler twins next door.

But Bobo had messed up both our beds now, and was starting to fuss: "When will the Freds be back? What's for supper? I'm hungry—can I have a snack? Will there be snacks when we go home? Can I take my teddy bear? The Freds will go home with us, right? Right?"

"Let's go to the park," I said. "I'll push you on the swing."

Bobo tucked his hand into mine, and we stepped out the front door.

"Don't want to move away from Fredtown," he whispered. "Don't want to move *anywhere.* Even home."

It was like some evil fairy godmother had cast a spell on the little boy who'd so gleefully jumped up and down on his bed only moments earlier. In the blink of an eye, he'd turned into a child who might cry at the brush of dandelion fluff against his cheek; at the scrape of a shoe against his heel; at a single wrong word from me.

"Hey," I said in my strongest voice. I made myself forget for a moment that I was worried about going home too. "Hey—look at me!"

Bobo turned his head and looked. A small almost-tear trembled in his eyelashes.

"No matter what, you will have me with you, remember?" I said. "Your big sister, who's been with you always? Doesn't that matter more than where we live? People matter more than places or things. You know that."

"I know that," Bobo repeated.

The almost-tear didn't fall. But he didn't wipe it away, either.

"Okay, race you to the park!" I said, and took off, tugging on his hand.

It was perfectly safe to dash off without watching where we were going. There were stop signs at all the cross streets along the boulevard. Fredtown was designed like that, to have as many places as possible to run and play.

I told myself we were running just to get Bobo to leave

his sad thoughts behind. But maybe I wanted to run away a little bit, too.

I let Bobo beat me to the park, and he was already swinging on the monkey bars by the time I got there. I pretended to huff and puff, making my final strides into huge, dramatic events, just like our Fred-daddy always did.

"Can't . . . take . . . another . . . step," I panted, totally hamming it up. "Oh, wait. . . . Almost . . . there. Almost . . ."

I made my steps gigantic and labored, as if I had only enough energy for one or two more.

Bobo giggled, just like I'd hoped.

"You're silly, Rosi," he called to me, dangling from the metal bars. "Watch!"

He kicked his legs forward, building momentum to reach for the next rung of the monkey bar. He'd just learned to swing all the way across the bars. Fred-mama, Fred-daddy, and I had all stood there and clapped for him his very first time, only last week.

And now it was my turn to have tears stinging my eyes. Those were the same monkey bars I'd first conquered when I was about Bobo's age. I could remember Fred-mama and Fred-daddy clapping for me, too, standing in the exact same spot. Every memory I had was like that—located in Fredtown. My whole life had happened here: either on the sun-splashed playground; or in the bright, open, cheery school; or in the marketplace aisles, crowded with a world of treasures; or at our house, where Fred-mama and Fred-daddy took turns tucking Bobo and me into our beds. . . .

Why didn't they just tell us to call Fredtown "home," and never make us move anywhere else? I thought rebelliously. I slashed the back of my hand against my eyes, wiping away the tears. Or at least hiding them. *Why didn't they just tell us our Fred-parents were our real parents and left it at that? Why did they even have to mention our other parents? How much could those real parents of ours actually care if they never contacted us?*

There were other little kids on the playground, other big brothers and sisters watching carefully nearby. On a normal day, I probably would have taken charge and suggested some game everyone could play; I would have gotten busy counting off teams and doling out playground balls and appointing umpires or referees. Or maybe I would have gathered the younger kids together for a giggly session of shared jokes and riddles and silly made-up stories. But I didn't like the way the eight- and nine- and ten-year-olds were watching me now— like they thought *I* had answers; like they thought I might be able to explain what it meant that we were going home.

I kept one eye on Bobo but took a step back from the playground. I pretended I was so deep in thought that it would be wrong for anyone to interrupt me. Cupping my chin in my hand, I gazed down into one of the town hall window wells—that was what we called the dug-out spaces around the basement windows. The spaces were only about two feet by two feet, just deep and wide enough to let light in. You might think the window wells would also be great places for little kids to slip down into during hide-and-seek games, but they were too obvious, the first places any seeker looked. So mostly we all just avoided them.

Only, there was a little girl hiding in this window well now.

It was a little girl whose moss-green dress might as well have been camouflage, especially matched with her dark hair and dusky skin. All those shadowy colors blended in with the dappled light and pebbles and fallen leaves at the bottom of the window well. Still, I crouched down and tapped the little girl's back.

"Cana!" I whispered. "Quick—go hide somewhere else, someplace harder to find. . . ."

I was surprised that this particular little girl would make such a careless mistake. Cana was only five, like Bobo, but she was unusually quick and sturdy and smart. She'd probably had all the founding principles of Fredtown memorized even before she started kindergarten: *The arc of the moral universe is long, but it bends toward justice.* And *For to be free is not merely to cast off one's chains, but to live in a way that respects and enhances the freedom of others.* And *A small body of determined spirits fired by an unquenchable faith in their mission can alter the course of history. . . .*

See what I mean? Not easy words, not easy thoughts. But Cana was good at remembering.

She turned and peered up at me, her heart-shaped face tilted just so.

"Oh, I'm not playing hide-and-seek," she whispered back. "I'm listening. Edwy told me to."

I glanced past Cana, toward the blurry, distorted shapes behind the glass-block basement window. Everything fell into place. Those blurry shapes were Freds. They were having their meeting in the town hall basement.

And Edwy had bribed or tricked or swindled Cana into eavesdropping for him. Into spying.

"But that's—that's—," I sputtered, too angry to explain. I held out my hand to Cana. "Here. Let's get you out of there before you get in trouble."

And before Edwy lets you take all the blame if you get caught, I thought.

Cana took my hand and I pulled her up. She stood on the brink of the window well and wrinkled her tiny face into a confused squint.

"We're allowed to hide there," she said. "I wasn't breaking any rules."

"Except that it's wrong to eavesdrop on the Freds," I said,

still crouched beside her. "We're not allowed to hide there when the Freds are meeting."

"Why?" Cana asked. "And why not?"

"Because we're children and they're adults," I said. "Because there are things we're not allowed to know yet." I'd spent my entire life in a town where practically every other kid was younger than me. I could answer "Why?" and "Why not?" questions in my sleep. But this time I couldn't stop myself from asking another question of my own. "But since you did eavesdrop . . . what did you hear?"

I need to know so I can decide whether to tattle on Edwy, I told myself. *I have to know if Cana heard anything damaging, that would require her to see a counselor to banish dangerous images from her mind. I need to know because . . .*

Because I was every bit as curious as Edwy.

That was the honest reason.

Cana tilted her head and gazed at me.

"Nothing *interesting*," she said. "Edwy said the interesting stuff would be anything that was opposite what they told us, and there wasn't any of that."

Edwy thinks the Freds are lying, I decided. *Does he think we're not really going home? Not really going to meet the parents we've never known?*

"So they just said stuff you already knew?" I asked Cana. She shrugged.

The Freds kept talking about how we're all so innocent and trusting," she said, blinking up at me. *She* certainly looked innocent and trusting.

She's five, I thought. *She* is *innocent and trusting. That's how Edwy could trick her without really even trying. And . . . so could I.*

I sighed and started to reach out to Cana, to pat her back reassuringly and tell her to run off and play with Bobo and the other little kids. But she wasn't done talking.

"One of the Fred-daddies said maybe they'd raised us to be too trusting," she said. "He said . . ." She rolled her eyes skyward, as if searching her memory for the exact words she'd overheard. "He said maybe they'd just been setting us up for disaster all along."

Disaster?

The word hit me like a thunderbolt. For a moment I felt like I'd had the air knocked out of my lungs.

Then I saw the way Cana peered at me, so anxiously. I didn't know if she'd understood what she'd heard when she heard it, but she understood now.

Probably because of the way I reacted.

"I'm sure he was only joking," I said quickly. "Exaggerating. To be silly. Or talking about some kind of game. You know how some kids act like it's a disaster to get tagged out in Wiffle ball. Edwy does that."

"Oh," Cana said, wrinkling her nose. "I didn't think of that."

She stood before me, a little girl in a moss-green dress. A little girl who was too smart to believe what I'd just said.

"Just don't eavesdrop anymore," I said. "It's too easy to hear something that might just confuse you. Or upset you. For no reason."

Cana still looked doubtful. I put my arm around her and led her toward the playground, toward the monkey bars where Bobo was playing.

If any of the Freds glanced out from the town hall just then, would they see two innocent girls, the older one looking after the younger, like she was supposed to?

Or would they see a whole park full of children headed for disaster?

CHAPTER THREE

"**Last bag**," Fred-mama said, easing my suitcase onto the back of the truck that was taking everyone's belongings to the airport.

"Thanks," the driver called back to her. He went on to the next house, where the Fred-parents of the toddler twins Peki and Meki started loading up.

"That *was* everything, wasn't it?" Fred-mama asked me.

"Except for what you gave me to carry myself," I said, turning around so she could see the little knapsack already strapped to my back. I'd peeked inside: It held a book to read on the plane, and lots of extra sandwiches and snacks. I'd seen Fred-mama pack a bulging knapsack for Bobo as well.

"Good," Fred-mama said. But she didn't whirl around to head back inside to gather up Bobo and Fred-daddy, to get us all moving toward the airport. She just stood there, so I just stood there too.

"Mama," I whispered, and it was the first time in my life I had ever addressed her that way.

"*Fred*-mama," she corrected me, in that same gentle-but-firm tone she'd used with me my whole life. "I'm only your Fred-mama. Your real mama is waiting for you at home."

"*You're* my real mama," I said. "You. Not anyone else."

It was like I had no choice: Either I had to spit out the angry words inside me or they would make me collapse; they would weigh me down and pin me to the ground, and I would never be able to get up.

"How can someone be a mama when she hasn't seen me in twelve years?" I asked. "When she's never even come to visit? How can you send Bobo and me—and all the other kids—back to a place we've never been? *And* expect us to call that strange place home?"

"Oh, honey," Fred-mama said, wrapping her arms around me.

I buried my face against her shoulder. Fred-mama was wearing a dress I'd once told her was my favorite: It was soft cotton with a pattern of lilac sprigs. When I was younger, I used to study it and tell her which flower cluster I liked best; I used to ask if someday, when I was a grown-up lady, I could get a dress like that, too.

I expected the feel of that soft, familiar fabric against my face to be the only comfort possible. I expected Fred-mama to offer me nothing but a hug and the same empty phrases the Freds had been giving us all along: *You're too young for us to explain everything. Someday, when you're a grown-up, you'll understand.*

But Fred-mama took in a gulp of air that didn't sound comforting, confident, gentle, or firm.

"Oh, Rosi," she whispered into my hair. "You're the one I feel sorriest for. Well, you and Edwy. Because you two are old enough to understand that something's wrong."

I pushed away from her shoulder so I could stare her straight in the face.

"I am?" I said. "We are? Then tell me—"

Fred-mama began shaking her head. The motion looked regretful, apologetic. And a little sneaky. Her dark curls bounced against her cheeks, and her eyes darted about, scanning the quiet street. It was like she was checking to make sure Peki and Meki's parents had finished loading the truck and gone back inside their house (they had); she was checking to make sure the truck had turned the corner and driven away toward the airport.

It had, too. Except for us and the row of towering trees out in the boulevard, the street was empty.

"I'm sorry," Fred-mama said. "I'm not allowed to tell you anything else. This is all very . . . complicated. But I know you can tell this isn't how things were supposed to be. Not what we intended. Things . . . changed. All of us Freds—we want the best for you. Your parents undoubtedly want the best for you too."

There was something in her voice I'd never heard before, something she'd never before let her guard down to reveal. Was it fear? Anguish? Grief?

It sounded like she was trying to convince herself, as much as me, that what she was saying was true.

"I don't even know my parents!" I said frantically. "They haven't seen me since the day I was born! How can they know what's best for me? How can they know anything about me?"

Fred-mama kept shaking her head.

"I'm sorry," she said. "So, so sorry. But . . . just remember. You are a good person. You'll remember everything we've taught you."

What was she really trying to tell me?

The door of our house opened just then, Fred-daddy stepping out onto the porch. He had Bobo perched on his shoulders, and the two of them had to duck down so Bobo didn't hit his head on the doorframe.

"It's time," Fred-daddy said, and I could hear the strain in his voice too—the strain he was undoubtedly trying to hide for Bobo's sake.

Did he also feel sorry for me? If Bobo hadn't been there,

would Fred-daddy have dropped the pretense, just like Fred-mama had? Could the three of us have wept on one another's shoulders? And spoken freely?

It was useless to wonder about what-ifs. Bobo *was* there. Bobo was always there for me to think about; I was always responsible for my little brother. I would be more responsible for him than ever, now that we were going home.

"Ready for our big adventure?" I asked him. I tilted my head back to gaze up at him, perched high above me on Fred-daddy's shoulders. I made my voice artificially excited, too, as if I was thrilled by the events ahead of me and Bobo should be too.

I knew my duty.

Fred-mama patted my shoulder. The pat still held a lingering sense of apology, but it mostly just said, *Thank you. Thank you for protecting Bobo. Thank you for being such a good big sister. Thank you for letting us know we can count on you.*

We started walking toward the airport.

Other kids and Freds spilled out of the houses we passed. It became like a parade, or a flowing river containing every resident of Fredtown.

I had never seen so many people—or, especially, so many kids—walk so quietly. For one long stretch, I could hear nothing but kids' knapsacks thudding against their backs; it made me think of the sad tolling of bells. Even the youngest babies seemed to understand that something strange and awful was happening. They rode in their Fred-parents' arms, clutching onto sleeves and fingers; all the babies seemed to be looking around with huge eyes, as if somehow they knew they had only a little more time left to gaze upon the loving faces they'd learned so recently. Most of the children in the toddler-to-kindergartner range were like Bobo, perched on Fred-parents' shoulders. It was like some picture Edwy and I might have seen in social studies class, like watching a procession of solemn young rajas swaying atop the backs of elephants. Except these young rajas held on so tightly.

None of them are going to want to let go when they get to the airport, I thought.

Neither would the elementary school kids walking alongside their Fred-parents, holding their Fred-parents' hands.

Neither would I.

I walked without touching anyone, but I could still *feel* Fred-mama and Fred-daddy on either side of me. We were separated by only a few centimeters and a scant scattering of air molecules—that was *nothing*. I had never been apart from them before for longer than a school day or an overnight at a friend's house. And even then, I had always known that they were close by, that they would be there instantly if I got hurt or needed them for any other reason. How would this work when they stayed here and Bobo and I went home? How far away would I have to be before I knew I'd lost them?

"Rosi and Bobo! Two of my favorite children!"

We were passing the school; the principal, Mrs. Osemwe, was standing out front, passing out hugs. If I'd been paying attention, I probably would have heard her calling the kids in front of us favorites, too. That was one of the things Edwy mocked—the way Mrs. Osemwe and all the teachers used that word for everyone.

"'Favorite' is supposed to mean you like someone best," he'd argued, back when we were still speaking to each other. "For there to be a favorite, there has to be someone you like *less*. Someone you maybe even hate."

"Nobody would *hate* another person," I'd told Edwy, too scandalized by his use of that ugly word to dwell on technical definitions.

But now, letting myself be wrapped into Mrs. Osemwe's pillowy arms, I noticed that she held on exactly long enough to make me feel comforted. She knew me so well. Pulling away, I met her kind, gentle gaze before she moved on to hugging children behind us—again, in the exact right way. She didn't have to say or do anything else for me to know Edwy was wrong. It *was* possible for Mrs. Osemwe to view every single one of the children of Fredtown as her favorite. She had enough love for all of us. All the adults in Fredtown did.

What would we do without them?

I stumbled on. It seemed like no time at all before we reached the airport: a long, flat, open field—the runway—and a single simple barnlike terminal. Planes rarely flew in or out of Fredtown, so people commonly gathered around to watch anytime such a miraculous event occurred. I could tell myself that today was no different than any other Special Delivery Day. I could pretend that I was just going to watch a plane land and a dignitary or a bunch of cargo handlers step off—or on— and then I would go back to my ordinary life.

But if I was just here to watch planes and dignitaries and cargo, and nothing was going to change, everyone around me would be shouting and exclaiming. Probably singing and dancing, too.

Everyone around me stayed silent.

No—the younger children around me were starting to whimper and whine.

"No," Bobo said quite suddenly, and it occurred to me that this could be his answer to my question way back at our house: *Ready for our big adventure?*

I wanted to tell him, *Oh, me neither, Bobo. Let's you and me just stay here. Let's not go anywhere. Let's not have anything change.*

I saw that my Fred-daddy was trying to lift Bobo off his shoulders and Bobo was digging in his heels, tightening his grip.

"Here, Bobo," I said, reaching for him as I switched my knapsack to one side. "I bet Fred-daddy's back is getting tired. Why don't you ride your sister-horsy for a while instead?"

Bobo looked back and forth between our Fred-daddy and me. He stuck out his lower lip.

"Stand on my own," Bobo demanded, distrust in his voice.

Our Fred-daddy put Bobo down on his own two feet. Bobo immediately dived for our Fred-daddy's legs and coiled his arms around Fred-daddy's knees.

Part of me wanted to do the exact same thing.

Fred-mama crouched down beside Bobo.

"You're a big boy," she said. It sounded like she was holding back tears. Could Bobo hear that in her voice too?

"We've raised you to be strong and true and kind to others," Fred-mama went on. She patted Bobo's back. "You have to think about your parents, about how much they've missed you, about how happy they'll be to see you again. You have to be kind to them."

It sounded like Fred-mama was having a hard time thinking about being kind to our real parents.

"Come with us," Bobo wailed, his face against Fred-daddy's

leg. "*Some* of the Freds are going home with us."

I waited for Fred-mama or Fred-daddy to deny this, but they didn't.

Now, how did Bobo know that? I wondered.

"It's only the Freds who meet certain criteria," Fred-daddy said helplessly. "The ones whose children are particularly . . ."

"Vulnerable," Fred-mama finished for him. Her face twisted with more misery than I had ever seen on anyone's face.

Normally, our Fred-parents would have defined a big word like that for Bobo, but neither of them attempted that now.

"The fact that Fred-mama and I aren't allowed to go— that just means the people in charge know that you and Rosi are strong and capable," Fred-daddy added. "And you have each other."

"Don't want to be strong," Bobo wailed, still clutching Fred-daddy's leg. "Want to stay with you!"

I wanted to cry with him. I wanted to throw myself to the ground and pound my fists on the dirt and scream at the top of my lungs. I wanted to act like a five-year-old too. Maybe even a baby.

You can't, I told myself. *You and Edwy are the oldest kids in Fredtown. You have to set a good example.*

I glanced around, suddenly curious to see how Edwy was dealing with all this. He was probably standing a cold, careless distance away from his Fred-parents; he was probably slouching and shrugging and rolling his eyes.

I couldn't see Edwy or his Fred-parents anywhere nearby, and the crowd was packed too tightly to see very far out. And now the commotion was overwhelming. All the adults must have started their good-byes at the same time as my Fred-parents, because just about every kid I could see was screaming and crying and wailing and desperately hugging.

And yet somehow, above all that noise, I could hear another sound: an airplane engine zooming closer and closer. I looked up, fixing my eyes on one dark speck in the blue, blue sky. The speck grew bigger and bigger; it transformed from a speck into an evil winged creature. Then it dropped from the sky and rocketed across the runway toward all of us kids and Freds. The engine noise became overpowering; it drowned out the screams, the cries, the weeping.

Then the plane came to a stop and lowered a set of stairs. The engine noise stopped, too. Maybe there were still kids crying; maybe Bobo was still wailing at the top of his lungs right beside me. But I didn't hear any of it. It felt like the whole world had gone silent and still and frozen, waiting for what came next.

A man stepped out of the plane, and—

He wasn't a Fred.

I'm not sure how I could tell, in that very first split second. He was dressed in dark pants and a loose white tunic— nothing a Fred wouldn't wear. He was an adult, and every adult I'd ever seen was a Fred. He had two arms, two legs, two eyes, two ears, one nose, and one mouth.

Maybe it was silly, but I checked these things, because I was trying to figure out what was different.

Was his face too rough? Were his eyes too hard? Was the curl of his lip a little too surly?

How could I look at a man and know right away that he wasn't a Fred?

The man at the top of the stairs held up something in his right hand—a piece of paper.

"There's been a change," he announced. He sounded triumphant, gloating. "We'll be taking only the children. All the Freds have to stay here."

Several of the Freds began protesting: "No!" "That's not fair!" "That's not what we agreed to!"

The man waved the paper at us as if it had magical powers to silence Freds.

"It's what your leaders agreed to," he said. "They had no choice. *You* have no choice but to obey."

Someone must have scrambled up the stairs to check it

out, but I couldn't really see. Something had gone wrong with my eyes. Or maybe the problem was my brain. All I could think was, *I'm going to a place with no Freds. No Freds at all.*

I didn't even know what the difference was between Freds and the type of adults my parents were. No one had ever explained. But I knew it had to be something big. The thought *No Freds, no Freds at all* . . . kept spinning in my brain, tangling my mind in knots.

And then I started noticing the hubbub around me again because Fred-mama was shouting in my ear: "You're going to have to watch out for Bobo *and* all the other little kids! Please, please, take care of them all . . . and yourself. . . ."

Fred-daddy thrust Bobo into my arms, and then we were all swept forward, shoved toward the airplane.

My arms wrapped automatically around Bobo, but I was so dazed and numb that Fred-mama had to help me hang on. She had to place one of my hands on Bobo's shoulder and one under his rear so he didn't slip out of my grasp.

"Make sure you put Bobo's seat belt on when you get on the plane!" Fred-daddy urged me. "Make sure you put on your own!"

Around me, other Fred-parents were telling their children, "Don't forget to brush your teeth every night!" "Remember to share your toys!" "Remember everything we've taught you!" "Remember to be good little children!"

Good little children, good little children, good little children . . .

I saw children crying and clinging to their Fred-parents' legs. I saw men yanking babies from their Fred-parents' arms. I turned back to my own Fred-mama and Fred-daddy—maybe to grab onto them as hard as I could—but the crowd surged just then, pushing Bobo and me up the stairs. I couldn't see my Fred-parents anymore. I hadn't even had a chance to tell them a proper good-bye.

"Wait!" Bobo screamed, squirming in my arms. "Have to tell—"

I couldn't even hear what it was that Bobo wanted to tell our Fred-parents. But it was too late. If I let go of Bobo, I might lose him too.

"They know you love them!" I yelled at Bobo, the crowd carrying us farther and farther away from our Fred-parents. "They understand whatever you were going to say!"

I stumbled onto the plane. Rows of seats stretched out before me. Little kids were falling down and getting stepped on. While Bobo clung to my neck, I reached down and pulled up Nita, one of the ten-year-olds, who was crying on the floor.

"Help the little kids into their seats and buckle them in," I told her. "Then sit down and fasten your own seat belt."

The crowd pushed forward, so I didn't have time to see whether Nita did what I told her or not.

Eight-year-old Rosco was cowering in the row behind Nita's. He was sucking on his thumb. An eight-year-old!

"Help the littler kids," I told him. "Remember? That's what you're always supposed to do. Wherever you are, in Fredtown or going home."

I tried to sound like a Fred; I tried to make my voice hold the same quiet authority a Fred voice always contained. And maybe it worked, because Rosco popped the thumb out of his mouth and said, "Oh. Okay."

In the last glimpse I caught of him he was turned around, easing his little brother, Rono, into one of the seats.

I kept going down the aisle. There was still a part of me that wanted to scream and cry and pound my fists on the ground—or run back and grab onto Fred-mama and Fred-daddy and refuse to leave. Or maybe even suck my thumb like Rosco. But it helped a little to try to keep my voice calm; to focus on soothing the smaller children, drying their tears, lifting them into their seats, getting them to assist one another. By the time we were about halfway down the aisle, Bobo was walking alongside me instead of clinging to my neck; he was like my little assistant, a five-year-old telling four- and three-year-olds how their seat belt buckles worked. It made my heart swell a little with pride.

See? I told myself. *We'll be okay. Everything's going to be okay.*

Those were the words I began passing out, intoning them as I moved down the aisle.

Then I got to a row of seats that looked empty until I was right beside it.

Edwy was crouched down in that row. He had the cushioned covering pulled back from the seat, and he was using a nail to scratch something into the metal below. Maybe it was just an ordinary drawing.

No. Knowing Edwy, it was probably something bad.

"Couldn't you help?" I demanded. "Just this once, couldn't you do something useful? Couldn't you *try* to be a better role model? Two hundred crying children around you, and you—you—"

I gestured helplessly. Words didn't exist to tell Edwy what I thought of him.

Edwy's face flushed, and he peered up at me from beneath his dark cap of curly hair. His green eyes narrowed. I remembered that he and I hadn't spoken directly to each other in more than a year.

"Really?" he said. "They think we should sit down and shut up and not even make a peep while they ruin our lives. And you want me to help?"

It was my turn to go red in the face. I could feel it.

"Oh, and what you're doing is better?" I asked.

Bobo tugged on my hand.

"Are you and Edwy fighting?" he asked. His tears, never completely dried to begin with, threatened to come back.

"No, no," I said quickly. "Edwy and I are just . . . *discussing*. Discussing is good, remember?"

Edwy snorted. I fixed him with a steely glare, alternating with quick glances down toward Bobo's head. Even Edwy should have been able to tell that I was telegraphing, *Please don't say anything to make Bobo or anyone else cry again.* Even Edwy should have been able to understand why we didn't want every kid on the plane sobbing all the way home.

"Fine," Edwy said.

He scrambled up into his seat and clicked the seat belt into place around his waist. He crossed his arms and squeezed his eyes shut. Then he squirmed a little and yelled out, "Everyone, this is how you're supposed to behave."

A second later he was completely still again, an unseeing, unmoving crossed-arm statue.

"Yeah, thanks a lot, *Edwy*," I muttered. "So nice of you to help."

I was counting on Edwy to hear the sarcasm in my voice—and counting on Bobo to be too young to notice.

I couldn't deal with Edwy just then.

I stepped on down the aisle to the next row of crying, terrified children who needed my help.

It was only later, when we were buckled in and about to take off, and I was whispering to Bobo, "We're fine, we're fine, we're going home and you'll love it there, everything's going to be okay," that I let myself think of Edwy again. The image popped into my mind of him sitting like a statue, a smirk frozen on his face. Except—he hadn't actually stayed perfectly still. There had been the slightest movement in the corner of his eye. Had it been a tic? A twitch? A mostly hidden wink?

Or was it a tear?

Had Edwy been crying too?

CHAPTER FOUR

"**Where is home?**" Bobo asked.

We were taking off; I had to rip my attention away from the window to answer him.

"It's over the mountains and across the sea," I said. "Remember? You learned about it in school."

I could have told him all sorts of names just then: *Atlantic, Pacific, Amazon, Nile, Kilimanjaro, Everest, Denali* . . . I could have taught him the geography of the entire planet. I could have told him tidbits about all sorts of places: how the golden rice he loved to eat came from the Philippines and Taiwan and America; how the Freds had taken their name from the Norwegian word for peace, since a famous peace prize was given out in Norway. But I didn't say anything else, because I didn't want to miss my last glimpse of Fredtown.

It looked so small now.

A moment ago we'd been on the ground, and just our one moment of traveling had made the crowd of Freds at the airport shrink down so completely that I had to squint to be sure they were still there. Then Fredtown was just tile roofs and leafy trees and the grid of streets; then the streets and the trees and the roofs seemed to merge, and the only feature I could make out for sure was the broad smear of green in the middle of Fredtown that had to be the park.

"I want to see!" Bobo said, tugging on my arm.

Just one moment, I thought. I just wanted one moment to myself, to feel my own feelings and think my own thoughts. And to say good-bye in my own way.

But I sat back so Bobo could see out the window too. He strained forward against his seat belt.

"Clouds," he said. "We're swimming in clouds."

I looked again—he was right. Fredtown was too far behind us to see anymore, and now we were surrounded by what seemed to be white cotton batting. From school, I knew the clouds were just water vapor, but it looked like we could step out the window onto the nearest cloud; it looked like we could bounce and tumble and jump from cloud to cloud like they were the greatest playground ever.

Maybe we would do that, all us kids from Fredtown. Maybe we'd just stay in the clouds and play forever. And never go home.

A sudden gap opened in the clouds, and I gasped.

"Oh, look, Bobo, it's the Old One," I said. "The mountain

we always see far off in the distance from Fredtown—this is what it looks like from above."

Below us, the mountain was a mottled green and brown—no, those were just shadows from the clouds. My eyes were playing tricks. The mountain itself was solid rock, strong and enduring, a gentle watchman who'd stood by Fredtown for as long as anyone could remember. I blinked back tears—I hadn't thought I'd get this one last glimpse. If I could, I wouldn't stay and play in the clouds; I'd stay and gaze at the Old One.

"Take it with us," Bobo demanded. "Take Old One, too!"

He was working himself up to a tantrum; with a little more air in his lungs, he could have become hysterical.

"Don't worry, Bobo," I said, putting my arm around him. "There's a mountain waiting for us at home, too. It's just got a different name. Remembrance. Can you say that?"

"'Membrance," Bobo muttered, making the word sound sad and ominous.

The plane jerked just then, seeming to jump a few feet higher in the sky for no reason. I'd never been on a plane before; was this normal? All around us, kids started shrieking. I expected the pilot or one of the other adults to speak over the intercom system and calm everyone down, but that didn't happen.

I unbuckled my seat belt and stood up.

"Everyone! Everyone! Stop screaming!" I yelled in my loudest voice, trying to make it carry over shrieks and sobs and moans. I tried to figure out what a Fred might say. "We're fine! It's just turbulence! Planes do that sometimes. Just keep your seat belts on and everything will be okay!"

I think some of the kids around me heard and settled down, but I was near the back of the plane; the kids at the front would have had to be terrified.

I took a step toward the aisle.

And *then* the PA system crackled to life. There was a sound like static, and then a man's angry voice said, "Girl in the back, *sit down* and put your seat belt back on. How dumb are you? Do you want to be killed?"

Did he just call me dumb? I thought numbly. *Dumb? He did. He really did.*

"Dumb" was one of those words that could only be used for objects or animals—a dog might be called, sympathetically, a "poor dumb beast." Or someone who was really mad might say, "My dumb pencil broke." But all the adults in Fredtown had drilled into us that we should never call another child dumb; no matter how furious we got, we were never allowed to blurt out, "Well, you're just dumb!"

Every now and then a kid slipped up, and that led to long, patient talks from one of the Freds about how awful it was to hurt another person's feelings.

How could an *adult* call someone dumb?

I wanted so badly to go to the man on the PA system and explain, *Yes, I know I'm putting my life at risk—a little bit—by taking my seat belt off and standing up. But I'm doing it for a good cause. I'm trying to soothe the little kids. That's brave and kind, not dumb.*

I wanted to defend myself against that awful label, "dumb." I thought that would have counted as standing up for my own rights. Not as being rude or disrespectful.

Then I realized Bobo was tugging on my arm and screaming hysterically, "Rosi, don't be killed! Please, please don't die!"

The little girl at the end of our row, six-year-old Aili, was screaming, "Don't want anyone killed! Want to go back to Fredtown!"

As far as I could tell, every kid on the plane was now screaming just as loudly as Bobo and Aili. Maybe even Edwy was. Maybe even I was. It was that word, "killed." It was like a match put to the dry tinder of the worries and fears and sorrow of leaving behind our Fred-parents and everything we'd ever known. It was like the whole plane had been engulfed.

I had to do something. I had to do something for all the kids, not just Bobo and Aili and the others near me.

"Shh, shh, don't worry," I told Bobo and Aili. I pulled my

arm away from Bobo's grasp. He cried even harder, but that couldn't be helped right now.

"Everything will be okay," I told Bobo and Aili. "I'm going to fix this."

It took a lot of courage, but I stepped out into the aisle. I walked as quickly as I could toward the front of the plane, toward the little sectioned-off compartment where the adults—the non-Fred adults—were sitting.

Kids screamed louder as I passed, but I didn't stop. I just kept muttering, "Don't worry, don't worry, everything's going to be all right. . . ."

I was pretty sure nobody heard me. I kept going anyway.

The man on the PA system didn't say anything else, but as I neared the front of the plane, I could see one man facing backward, glaring out at me from the sectioned-off compartment. The closer I got, the more he glared. It was like walking toward storm clouds.

When I was about six rows away, the man shouted at me, "Are you a total idiot? Completely stupid? Sit *down!*"

I'd never heard the words "idiot" or "stupid" before, but from the way he said them, I guessed they was like "dumb," only worse. I guessed they were such horrible words that no one had been allowed to use them in Fredtown at all.

I kept walking.

"I can help you calm the children down," I said. "So they

don't cry for hours. So they're not traumatized."

The man gaped at me. He had gray, scruffy whiskers growing along his jawline. I couldn't decide if he wanted them to look that way or if he'd just been haphazard about shaving.

"I don't care if they cry," he said, shrugging. "That's what kids do. That's why we all brought earplugs." He popped something small and white out of one of his ears and held it up. Then he pointed over his shoulder into the compartment, where I could see what seemed to be stacked bassinets. Each one was labeled with a name, and contained a baby covered in tubes and wires. "And see? That's why the automatic tenders we have the babies in are soundproofed."

As he spoke, one of the babies began squirming and flailing his arms and legs. His face turned red. I couldn't hear anything, but he was clearly crying. Instantly a tube zoomed up to his mouth and he began sucking, even though tears still hung in his eyelashes.

I gasped.

"Babies need personal attention," I told the man. Maybe he just didn't know. "They need skin-to-skin contact, and—"

The man snorted.

"Oh, a little automation never hurt anyone," he said. "And it might kill me if I had to deal with crying babies for this whole trip. I wish the regulations let us put you all in isolation units. Little kids—ugh. But if the crying bothers you, well, I'm sure eventually they'll cry themselves to sleep. Then they'll be quiet."

This was like talking to Edwy. There were so many things wrong with what this man was saying, I didn't know where to begin.

"But, but . . ."

A lump was growing in my throat, a lump fed by being called "dumb" and "a total idiot." A lump that probably would have been there anyway from leaving the Freds behind, from seeing Fredtown and the Old One for the very last time. From having to shake Bobo's hand off my arm and walk away from him when he was scared and crying.

I tried to ignore the lump and talk past it.

"My idea was, if we go ahead and feed the kids early— like now—maybe they'll get distracted," I said. "They'll forget how sad they are and settle down."

Something in the man's face shifted. It looked like he wanted to laugh at me. Just to be mean, not because he thought something was funny.

"Oh, no," the man said. "I didn't sign on to provide food service for spoiled brats. I'm just the hired muscle. I'm just transporting cargo from one set of crazies to another. I'm not your parents. I'm not your precious Freds. Forget what I said about sitting down so you don't get your head bashed in from the turbulence. I don't care what you do. If you're too much of an idiot to follow simple orders, that's not my problem."

The whole time we'd been talking, I'd been standing in the aisle and the man had been leaning his head out from his compartment, where he was safely belted in. But now he pulled his head back and slid shut a door I hadn't even known was there.

He was done talking to me.

If I wanted to keep talking to him, I would have had to tug the door back open—if it wasn't locked—and beg him to take his earplugs out again. And peer into his mean, laughing whiskered face.

I couldn't do any of that. Not when the lump in my throat kept growing and growing and growing.

I heard the roar of the screaming, panicked children behind me. I heard the thump of my own heart, sad and trampled and afraid. And I heard a whispering voice in my mind that sounded a bit like Edwy's:

The Freds would never have hired a man like that. They wouldn't. So . . . does that mean it was our own parents who hired him and the other men?

If that's the kind of man our parents hired to take care of children, what are our parents like?

CHAPTER FIVE

We kept flying. The Freds had told us we would fly through
darkness and back into light, but even they hadn't been sure
exactly how long the trip would take—or how long it would
seem. I knew about time zones; I knew daytime in one place
could be night in another, and traveling by plane could trick
you into feeling like your days and nights were mixed up. But
I hadn't understood how leaving Fredtown could make me
feel like we'd been yanked out of time entirely. Away from
everything normal.

*You still have all the other children of Fredtown here with
you,* I told myself. *They need your help. That's normal.*

After the whiskered man shut the door in my face, I
stood there, frozen, for a moment. Then I managed to
swallow the lump in my throat—mostly, anyway. I turned
around, stood at the front of the plane, and tried one of
the clapping games our Fred-teachers always used to start
music class.

Clap, clap, clap-clap-clap . . .

I was lucky the children of Fredtown were so well trained. Even sobbing, even bawling their eyes out, the kids in the rows nearest me managed to bring their hands together for a feeble response: *Clap, clap, clap-clap-clap . . . clap!*

The wailing seemed a little quieter, even at the back of the plane. I went on to our teachers' next clapping pattern: *Clap, clap, cla-claaaap, clap . . .*

This time the response seemed to come from practically every kid on the plane: *Clap! Clap!*

I could still hear sniffling and whimpering after that, but at least the loud wailing had stopped.

"Listen up, everyone," I said. "How many of you brought food?"

Hands went up. Because the seat backs were so high and some of the children were so small, there were probably some hands in the air that I couldn't even see.

But I could see two or three kids who kept their hands in their laps. Their faces were twisted with worry now; one little girl's chin trembled like she was just barely holding back a return of heartbroken wailing. I couldn't imagine that those kids' Fred-parents had sent them without food in their knapsacks—probably the kids had just lost track of where it was, or even dropped it in the hubbub back at the airport.

"Okay, if you don't have food, it's no problem," I said. "I'm sure everybody else has more than enough to share, for as many meals as we need. As soon as the plane levels off, take out your food, if you have it, and divide it into two piles: one, what you want to keep for yourself, and the other, what you would be willing to give away."

The girl with the trembly chin started biting her lip. I looked down at my hands, which were holding on to the seats on either side of me. I didn't really need to hold on anymore, did I? The plane hadn't jumped or jolted or swooped suddenly to the side in, oh, at least five minutes.

"Okay, I think the plane has leveled off enough that you can start dividing up your food now," I said. "Do I have any volunteers to help me pick up the extra food and pass it out to the kids without food?"

Lots of hands went up once again.

Over the next several hours I passed out food and water bottles, I took little kids to the bathroom, I tucked blankets around drowsy toddlers longing for naps, I sang lullabies. After some of the kids started complaining about being thirsty, I found a little kitchenette at the back of the plane stocked with huge water jugs, so I could refill drinks. I had help with all those tasks—I deputized every kid over the age of seven except for Edwy. And even Edwy got a bunch of kids involved in a card game of some sort, so I guess he was keeping them from crying. At least he was doing that.

The adults never came out of their compartment. They kept their door shut.

It was just as well.

Finally, long after the whole plane had slipped into darkness, there came a moment when I was sure every other Fredtown child was sound asleep. I walked down the aisle one last time, glancing at sisters and brothers cuddling together, preschoolers holding on to toddlers' hands, big kids slouched down so smaller children could use their shoulders as pillows. And then I slipped back into my own seat beside Bobo. I slid Bobo's head onto my lap, and he sighed in his sleep, relaxing his body completely.

I looked out the window into darkness—the stars the only points of light, millions and millions of kilometers away. Light-years away. Back in Fredtown I'd always loved gazing at the night sky; I'd loved imagining myself as an astronaut zooming off into space. But now the stars made me feel lonely. Fredtown and my Fred-parents seemed so far away.

What would the entire town do without its children?

What would our hometown and our real parents be like, after so many years without us?

The lump in my throat came back, and the stars blurred. I allowed one silent, lonely tear to slide down my cheek.

Everything will be okay once we're actually home, I told

myself, just as I'd told Bobo, just as I'd been reassuring panicky children all day.

I imagined how we'd land at the airport, and kind grown-ups—maybe not Freds, but people like them—would gently escort us into some sort of waiting area. They'd speak to us in soft voices and feed us the kinds of food you get when you're sick or in need of particular comfort: chicken noodle soup, soft rice, ice cream. Invalid food. And then, quietly and in an orderly manner, they'd call for each set of siblings to meet their parents, to be welcomed and hugged and loved. . . .

Somebody tapped me on the shoulder.

Hastily, I brushed away the one tear on my cheek—though maybe now there was more than one. I turned my face away from the window, toward whoever had touched me.

It was Edwy.

In the darkness, his face was shadowed, his eyes hidden. I knew it was him by the shape of his head, by the fact that he was the only kid on the plane who was nearly the same height as me.

"Whatever happens," he whispered, "whatever our parents and home are like, you can't believe any lies. You and me, we've got to think for ourselves."

"That's what the Freds taught us," I whispered back.

"No—" Edwy shook his head, as if my answer had annoyed him.

Yeah, well, pretty much everything you've done for the past year has annoyed me, I wanted to say. But I didn't, because I didn't want to ruin this moment—Edwy actually talking to me seriously, like we always used to.

Both of us went silent for an instant, and then Edwy said, "You're not dumb, Rosi. You're smart. Don't listen to anyone who tries to tell you different."

"I wasn't going to," I said. In spite of myself, a bit of sarcasm had crept into my voice. To make up for it, I added, "You're smart too, Edwy,"

That was probably was the kindest thing I'd said to him in a year. Of course, it was practically the *only* thing I'd said to him in a year.

"We'll watch out for each other, right?" Edwy said.

I thought about how he'd gotten Cana to spy on the Freds for him back at the town hall. I thought about how he'd vandalized his airplane seat instead of helping the little kids. I thought about how he'd let me face the whiskered, mean laughing man all by myself.

But I still said, "Of course."

CHAPTER SIX

We were landing.

"Look out your windows, everyone," I called, straining against my seat belt so I could raise my head high and project my voice as far toward the front of the plane as possible. "That's home!"

"It looks like Fredtown!" someone called.

"Maybe they turned the plane around in the middle of the night and just flew us back to Fredtown!" someone else cried hopefully.

I could see where that might lead.

"It's not Fredtown," I called, trying to make my voice as Fred-calm and Fred-firm as possible. "But it does look a lot like Fredtown. So we'll all feel at home at home."

Some of the kids giggled, which was exactly what I'd intended. I thought about adding a few more awkward "at homes" along with an "er, I mean . . . ," and acting really goofy and comical to drive them into genuine belly laughs. But I wasn't sure I could pull it off. I felt too homesick for Fredtown myself.

Did our hometown look that much like Fredtown from the air? I couldn't tell yet if it really was that similar, or if this was just what any town would look like from above. There was a patterned grid of streets and green, leafy trees, and the roofs seemed to be made of the same kind of reddish tile as back in Fredtown. But maybe all roofs, everywhere, looked like that from above.

And then we were lower to the ground and all I could see was the runway—the runway with a huge crowd beside it, surging toward us.

They're waiting for us, I told myself. *They're eager to see us.*

That should have made me feel welcome and loved, but my stomach jumped nervously, in a way that had nothing to do with the plane's wobbly flying.

The crowd seemed to be coming too close. The plane veered first to the left, then to the right; then it touched down. Before the plane even came fully to a stop, I could see hands reaching up against my window—*pounding* on our window, actually.

I turned my back to the window, to block Bobo and Aili from seeing out.

I was too late.

"I'm scared," Bobo told me, his fists pressed against his chubby cheeks. "Those people . . ."

"Must not understand the safety rules around planes." I finished Bobo's sentence briskly, before he ended with something worse. "I'm sure whoever runs the airport will tell them how they're supposed to behave."

I remembered the landing procedure I'd imagined: the calm, orderly disembarking, the peaceful waiting in a quiet room where we'd eat chicken noodle soup.

I could hear people screaming outside, "We want our kids! We want our kids now!"

Someone will calm them down, I thought. If nothing else, that whiskery man who'd been so mean to me would probably be mean to those people, too. It was probably part of his job to keep them away from us until they asked nicely.

I was kind of glad I was at the back of the plane, and Mr. Mean Whiskers and all the other grown-ups were up near the door.

It's like they're guarding it, I told myself. *Guarding us.*

The plane jerked to a stop. Nobody came out from the grown-ups' sectioned-off compartment at the front. The pounding on the windows and the sides of the plane got louder and louder, fiercer and fiercer. Could an airplane's windows actually break just from being hit by bare fists? I glanced out the window beside me, and faces were pressed against the glass—twisted, furious faces, so transformed by rage that they didn't even look human.

Airplane windows are too strong to break, I told myself, trying to hold on to calm, cool Fred-logic. *And of course our parents are human. Only humans can have human children.*

Bobo and Aili were sobbing again, totally terrified, but the screams from outside were so loud that I couldn't even hear the boy and girl right beside me. Probably every other kid on the plane was sobbing and shrieking and afraid too. I remembered what Fred-mama had told me right before we left Fredtown: *You're going to have to watch out for Bobo and all the other little kids! Please, please, take care of them all . . .*

I scooped Bobo up in my arms—there was no way I was leaving him behind, so close to the window-pounding and the scary faces—and I moved toward the aisle. Aili grabbed my leg, her grip so tight that I could feel her fingernails through my dress and tights. She pressed her face against me so hard that her big red hair bow dug into my stomach.

"I'm just going up to the front of the plane to get all the other kids to calm down," I told her, in a voice that trembled way too much to be soothing. "That's where the door is. Don't worry, no one can get in except through the—"

In the next second, I noticed for the first time that there was a door at the back of the plane, too—a door marked

EMERGENCY EXIT ONLY. I noticed it because it was shaking. I couldn't quite separate the sound of fists hitting that door from all the other banging and screaming and crying around me, but I could almost feel the pounding like something inside me.

And then that back door to the plane sprang open, and a crowd of grown-ups—a *mob*—spilled into the plane.

I pulled back from the aisle and turned sideways so Bobo couldn't see around me. I hoped.

The mob of grown-ups streamed toward us, up the aisle, their greedy hands snatching children from the nearest seats. The chant "We want our kids! We want our kids now!" dissolved into cacophony, a disorienting blur of sound. It took a woman and a man shouting right beside my ear as they passed before I understood what had changed. Now all the grown-ups were calling out individual names.

"Lila!" the woman screamed. "Lila, Lila, Lila, Lila!"

The man yelled, "Breto? Gustine? Rechi?"

Were all the grown-ups calling for their own children?

"Aili?" a different man shouted in my ear.

My first thought was, *Hide her. Protect her. Don't let her be taken away. Not like this.*

I looked down to where Aili was clinging to my leg, her fingers glued to my tights and dress, her fingernails digging deep, her mouth open in a howl of fear. And maybe my glance betrayed her; maybe the man had seen photographs and recognized her. Suddenly his big hands were scooping Aili up, yanking her away.

Aili howled louder, a soaring cry of sheer terror.

I shifted Bobo's weight entirely to my left side and reached out with my right arm to hug Aili's shoulders. To comfort her. And pull her back.

"Stop!" I told the man. I tried to speak as loudly as possible. Could I make myself heard over the screaming? "You're scaring her! Children need calm, they need gentle explanations, they need . . ."

I looked straight into the dark eyes of the man who was holding Aili. His eyes narrowed cruelly. He pulled Aili out of my grasp and then even farther away, out of my reach.

Bigger and stronger and older should never use force to overpower smaller and weaker and younger, I thought.

But there was no way that I could say that and make myself heard, because the man was screaming at me, "This is *my* daughter! It's none of your business what I do to her!"

"But—," I said.

The man shoved my shoulder—fortunately, the right one, not the one that Bobo was cowering against. Bobo and I both fell against the top part of the seat behind us. An armrest dug into my leg, and I cried out.

Aili was still howling, her arms and legs flailing uselessly.

Powerlessly. The man jerked her even farther away from me and, using her body almost like a shield, cut his way through the crowded aisle back toward the door. The red bow from Aili's hair fell to the floor, and it was instantly trampled. And then, in the jumble of darting eyes and screaming mouths and other flailing children, both the man and Aili vanished from my sight.

I should have gone after Aili right away. I should have rescued her. I should have made myself heard—somehow. No one was stopping me.

Except that Bobo was clutching my shoulder and screaming just as hysterically as Aili. And if I waded into the crowd after Aili, wouldn't that just terrify him more?

I am my brother's keeper, I remembered. *I am always my brother's keeper.*

And he was younger than Aili. That made him even more vulnerable.

I looked back at Bobo's contorted, screaming face, and then at the mob of grown-ups stomping and lurching down the aisle, many of them now carrying wailing children.

This was chaos.

My ears rang with all the screaming—rang so badly, I couldn't even hear. The louder everyone screamed and cried, the more my head went silent. I remembered how horrifying our leave-taking from Fredtown had been, with the mean whiskered man and the other "hired muscle" people shoving us onto the plane. But that had been peaceful and orderly compared with this. That was the worst that Fredtown had to offer, the worst I'd ever encountered.

This was a stampede. This was a riot.

This was dangerous.

"Here," I said to Bobo as I gently slid us both down to the floor, down to the area between our seats and the ones in front of them. I wedged him against the side of the plane, using my own body as a wall to protect him from even seeing the chaos and the angry faces of the riot.

"We'll be safe here," I told him. "We just have to hide. That's all."

Who did I want that for the most? Him or me?

I tucked both our knapsacks around him like a blanket. Then I began to sing him a lullaby from when he was really tiny: *"Sleep, little baby, for you are safe / Sleep, little baby, for you are loved . . ."*

I couldn't hear my own voice, but the more I sang, the more I could remember how our Fred-parents had always sung that lullaby. Bobo curled against me, his face buried against my chest. He'd stopped shaking with sobs. Maybe he'd even stopped sobbing.

As long as I kept singing, I could tune out the screaming and the pounding feet behind me. But if I stopped to take a breath, I could hear it all again. The floor quaked beneath us, and I dared to glance around. I could only take in pieces of what I saw: grasping hands, screaming mouths, angry eyes . . .

Someone could get seriously hurt from all that trampling, I thought. The image of a boot smashing down on Aili's fallen red bow came swimming back into my mind. Children were more fragile than bows. More breakable. I didn't want to think it, but my brain added, *Someone could get killed.*

I looked back at the mashed curls on Bobo's head and went back to singing "*Sleep, little baby, sleep, sleep, sleep . . .*"

Then someone grabbed my shoulder.

CHAPTER
SEVEN

I whirled around and found myself staring into a ruined face. I say "ruined" because that was how I saw it first: like a burned-down house, like a wrecked car. Something that couldn't be repaired. The eyelids sagged and the bags under the eyes sagged; the skin of the cheeks seemed to have melted and then, oddly, frozen into rivulets and channels. The left side of the mouth drooped. This was a face that could never smile, only frown. A face whose owner must have been sad forever.

"I found you," a voice croaked, and it took that for me to realize: This was a woman's face.

I saw that the woman was wearing a dress, or what had once been a dress. Perhaps the sporadic gray blobs down the front of it had originally been sprigs of flowers many washings ago. Or maybe it was just dirty.

"Bobo, Rosi—is there something wrong with you that you were left behind?" the woman asked. "Is there something wrong with my children?"

"My" children, I thought. *"My."*

Could this be our mother?

And her first thought was that there might be something wrong with us?

I straightened my back.

"I was protecting Bobo," I said. "Keeping him safe. And calm. He's only five. This is scary for him."

I sounded like Edwy claiming that some rule he'd broken was unfair anyway. I sounded cowardly.

My Fred-parents would want me to protect Bobo. Wouldn't my real mother want the same thing?

The woman grunted.

"Five is old enough to . . ." She shook her head and glared, as if it was my fault she'd started to say something she didn't want to. "I thought maybe you hadn't even come. I thought the plane was empty. . . . Stand up, both of you."

I glanced past the woman, toward the aisle. Surprisingly, I couldn't see anyone running or screaming or grabbing just then. Were Bobo and I the last ones left on the plane? Had all the other children of Fredtown been taken away?

Had I failed them all, trying to protect Bobo?

I obeyed the woman's orders and unfolded my legs. I shoved our knapsacks to the side and pulled Bobo up with me. We both stood up straight, in the tiny space between the airplane seats.

I towered over the woman, and she took a step back. Surprise registered in her gaze so strongly that even the sagging eyelids couldn't hide it.

"Why, you're already full growed," she said.

Grown, I wanted so badly to correct her. Even more, though, I wanted her to catch her mistake and correct herself. And then maybe she'd laugh, and it would turn out that that face could smile after all, and she'd explain, *I'm sorry! I'm just so giddy about seeing you, I can't think straight. My children! I love you!*

But the frown stayed on her face. Her hooded eyes stayed cold.

I decided that if she kept speaking with bad grammar, I wouldn't let myself hear it. I'd translate it to proper grammar in my head.

"You're older than the pictures they sent," she said. "Those were only black-and-white, and we couldn't tell. . . . I missed everything. All your growing-up years. Those . . . those other people . . . they raised you complete."

Like it was all my fault. Like I had kept her from seeing newer pictures of me. Like I had run away from home as a newborn, just to spite her.

"I'm only twelve," I said, defensive again. "And, like I said, Bobo's only five, so . . ."

The woman knelt down and reached out her hand to

touch Bobo's face. Bobo looked up at me, checking for what he should do. I gave the barest of shrugs. I should have said, *It's all right. You're safe now,* or *Be a good boy and hug your mama.* But I couldn't squeeze any words past the sudden lump in my throat. Especially not those.

"We still get to raise Bobo," the woman murmured. She twisted so she seemed to be speaking only to Bobo. "Oh, your father's going to be so proud of you. So happy to meet you."

Wouldn't he be happy to meet me, too?

Bobo's gaze darted back and forth between the woman and me, his eyes asking, *Shouldn't the scary part be over? Should I still be afraid? Aren't you going to protect me from her?*

I let out a breath I hadn't realized I'd been holding.

"Everything's okay, Bobo," I said gently, even though it felt like a lie on my tongue. "This is our real mother. We're going home with her."

The woman harrumphed, as if she could hear the doubt in my voice. But then she took Bobo by the hand, pulling him out into the aisle. I stuck close beside him, which meant that I blocked the way for the woman to walk toward the back door of the plane. She started toward the front instead, tugging Bobo with her. I snatched up Bobo's and my knapsacks and followed along. No way was I letting him out of my sight.

But the woman had a slow, halting gait, and Bobo

dawdled, glancing back after every other step to make sure I was still there. This meant I had too much time to think between my longer-legged strides.

What if I refuse to go with this woman? What if I say I don't think it is safe for me or Bobo? What would I say that was based on? Her appearance?

It was wrong to judge people based on how they looked.

Or would I say it's because she didn't know the right past participle form of "grow"? Or because she was nicer to Bobo than she was to me?

That made it seem like I was just jealous and petty and mean.

Anyhow, what else could Bobo and I do besides going home with this woman? Who could I appeal to? It was always parents who were supposed to protect their kids, parents you were supposed to tell if you were afraid. Or some other trustworthy adult. But no Freds had come with us. The mean whiskery man and his friends didn't even care if we had food. And anyway, I hadn't seen a single one of them since we landed. If they'd cared at all, they would have stopped the stampede of adults grabbing kids.

Bobo hesitated and glanced back at me beside the row of seats Edwy had sat in. I nodded reassuringly at Bobo, and he faced forward again and kept walking. I had to turn my head to the side to try to collect myself.

That's when I saw a paper crumpled on the floor in front of Edwy's seat.

It figures Edwy would leave trash behind, I thought. *It figures he wouldn't care about littering.*

I wanted to think of him that way. I didn't want to think that even Edwy might been overcome and snatched up like Aili was. I didn't want to think that this paper could be something he'd intended to hold on to that he'd lost, like Aili lost her red bow.

I leaned over to pick up the paper, and it wasn't a napkin or a sandwich wrapper. This paper felt stiff and official, and when I flattened it out, it held a long row of stern words in dark ink on the white paper:

Be It Known:

Under the terms of Addendum 468 to Agreement 5062, none of the people commonly known as "Freds" shall be allowed to return with the children. Their presence has been judged to be too provocative, and therefore dangerous. Instead, only those of the neutral third party hired to make the exchange shall be allowed to accompany said children. And all people of this neutral third party shall depart within twenty minutes of the last child being reunited with the last parent. As long as the parents and others of their ilk continue to meet the terms of Agreement 5062, they will then hold total sovereignty and control over . . .

The paper was torn, so I couldn't see what parents had control over. Their children, I guessed. This had to be the decree that had caused such panic back in Fredtown. Edwy being Edwy, he'd somehow managed to swipe a copy in all the chaos.

But who would think Freds *are dangerous?* I wondered. *And—provocative?*

I didn't know what that word meant, but it sounded like "provoke." The Freds always scolded Edwy for provoking trouble. *They* would never provoke anyone. They were always trying to stop trouble and resolve every problem in a peaceful way.

Does Edwy understand what this means? I wondered. *Did he see the rest of the decree, the part that was torn off?*

I remembered Edwy scratching graffiti into his airplane seat. It could have just been Edwy being Edwy, provoking trouble as usual.

But what if it's something important? I asked myself. *Something about the part of this decree that's missing?*

Quickly, before I could change my mind, I darted toward the seat Edwy had sat in. I pulled back the cloth covering and the padding beneath, to find words carved crookedly into the metal frame.

I made out the first part: HEY, WORLD—

It figures Edwy would think the whole world should pay attention to him, I thought, allowing myself a wry smile.

But my smile faded when I deciphered the rest of the message:

THESE PEOPLE AREN'T REAL EITHER

CHAPTER EIGHT

Had Edwy meant that our real parents weren't real? That they weren't really ours, any more than the Fred-parents had been? How would he know that?

Or was he talking about somebody else entirely? The mean whiskery-faced man and his friends, maybe?

I felt a jolt of memory, a reminder of the time when Edwy and I stopped being friends. He'd said awful things about his Fred-parents—how could I trust anything he said about our real ones? Or any adult?

Edwy probably knew that I would get curious and eventually look at his graffiti. He was probably just messing with me, the way he always did. He probably didn't know or understand any more than I did about Addendum 468 or Agreement 5062 or any of the weirdness around us.

I decided I couldn't let myself think about what Edwy may or may not have meant. But I did tuck the decree into my knapsack, alongside my book and the leftover food I still had.

We walked past the other rows of seats and down the steps from the airplane: first the woman, then Bobo, then me. We descended into a clump of other parents and kids fleeing the plane—other kids who had hidden, probably; other parents who had maybe waited until the worst of the riot had stomped past before wading into the crowd.

But all the commotion around us was like something happening in a dream, out of focus. I could barely get my eyes to scan properly to make sure it was safe to take the next step across the cracked tarmac.

Sometimes when you're scared, it's because you're making up things to be scared of in your own head. *The only thing we have to fear is fear itself.* I needed to focus on that principle of Fredtown. I needed to accept that Bobo and I were supposed to be here in our real hometown, with our real parents. I needed to make my brain stop thinking of the woman on the other side of Bobo as "the woman" and think of her as my mother instead.

The Freds would want you to ask her what she wants to be called, I told myself. *Mama? Mommy? Mother?*

How could I say any of those names to this woman?

My brain rebelled. My mouth did too. I stayed silent.

Behind me on the runway, I heard a roar—the airplane engine rumbling to life again.

All people of this neutral third party shall depart within twenty minutes . . . , I thought. I looked back, catching a glimpse of smirking faces in the windows as the plane sped past. Within seconds it took off. The mean whiskered man and the others like him had followed the rule.

Good riddance, I told myself. Those men hadn't been any help anyway. But I really wanted to scream, *No, wait! Take Bobo and me with you! Take us back to Fredtown!*

Bobo's hand crept into mine. I knew he'd done it to comfort himself, but it steadied me, too. Bobo's hand was so plump and warm and solid, so familiar in this unfamiliar place. As much as he could drive me crazy sometimes, he really was a sweet little boy. Maybe he *was* trying to comfort me.

The woman looked at Bobo's hand in mine.

"You baby him," she said, frowning.

Anger like I'd never felt before surged through me. She didn't even know Bobo; she didn't know me. We were in a strange place, even if it was supposed to be home now. She was a stranger, even if she was supposed to be our mother.

Did she expect me to yank my hand away from my own brother? To shove him away?

"He's only little," I said. "Little children need—"

Her hand darted out in a flash. I jerked back so the palm of her hand wouldn't collide with my face.

"Don't you tell me what my own child needs," she said. "Don't you sass me."

She looked at her hand, still raised; she looked at Bobo between us. She let her hand drop.

She almost slapped me, I thought. *Would she have slapped me if I hadn't moved?*

I reeled back, slammed by my own thoughts even though I'd dodged the slap of her hand. No adult had ever struck me—certainly not Fred-mama or Fred-daddy. Little kids, yes: There's that phase at two or three where some kids feel powerless, and they lash out by biting or hitting. The Freds had told me again and again how to deal with that: Older kids and adults must never, ever, ever hit back. Kids need to learn as soon as possible that hitting isn't the answer.

My face burned, stinging almost as badly as if I really had been hit. I blinked back the tears that sprang to my eyes. And yet what I kept thinking was, *Did Bobo see that woman try to hit me? Oh, please, let it be that he didn't see that. Don't let him know what happened. What almost happened. Don't let him ever think that an adult might hit* him. . . . *Don't let him be damaged by this.* . . .

I looked down, and Bobo's head *wasn't* turned toward me. His face and his eyes were pointed straight ahead. Maybe he hadn't heard what the woman and I had said—maybe for him it just blended in with the sound of children crying around us. Maybe he hadn't felt me jerking away from the woman.

I looked back at the woman. We had a procedure in Fredtown: Whenever you felt that someone had wronged you, you talked it over with a trusted adult, and then you talked it over with the person who'd offended you. And then, after all that, if you still felt the slightest bit upset, you repeated the whole process again and again, until you were just tired of being mad.

Edwy was the only person I'd ever been mad at that I hadn't done that with.

But I couldn't tell this woman, *You wronged me just now,* because Bobo might hear. I couldn't say, *You hurt my feelings and gave me the impression that you don't value my viewpoint, that you don't value me.* I couldn't say anything.

Fredtown felt farther away than ever.

Bobo stopped walking.

"That looks like a mask," he said. "Why would a building wear a mask?"

He pointed to a structure far ahead of us, which I had taken for the airport terminal. Maybe it was a row of stores instead. But I'd never seen stores like this: Where there should have been windows displaying the most tantalizing wares, this structure had interlocking metal bars across the front, keeping everybody out.

The metal bars didn't look like a mask to me. They looked like a cage.

"All the stores are shut down," the woman said. "It's a holiday. The day we get our children back. The day we've been waiting for for the past twelve years."

She shot a glance at me, as if she was daring me to argue.

"But to put a building in a *mask* . . . ," Bobo said. He could be like a dog with a bone sometimes. When he got an idea stuck in his head, it was the hardest thing in the world to talk him out of it. His expression brightened. "Is there going to be a party? Does everyone get to wear a costume?"

"You talking about those metal gates?" the woman asked. "That's so the stores don't get robbed while the owners are away. That's all. It's because of thieves."

"People aren't supposed to take things that don't belong to them," Bobo said in the singsongy voice he'd used for repeating rules and principles back in Fredtown.

"That's right," the woman said, patting his head.

We didn't need metal gates and cages to keep people from stealing back in Fredtown, I thought. I pressed my lips together hard so I wouldn't slip and actually say that.

Would the woman try again to slap me if I said anything?

"Now come along," the woman said, tugging on Bobo's arm. Her hand slid down his wrist; it looked like she wanted to hold his right hand while I held his left.

But Bobo pulled away. He cowered against me and whined, "My legs are tired. Carry me, Rosi."

We hadn't even walked the length of a soccer pitch—not even the miniature soccer pitches Bobo played on. I'd seen him run that distance, back and forth and back and forth, dozens of times without stopping. Without even breathing hard.

His legs couldn't have been tired, and normally I would have said so. I would have told him he was perfectly capable of walking on his own. Instead, I bent down and was about to pick him up when the woman said, "No, no, I'll carry you, Bobo. I haven't gotten to carry you since the day you were born."

I thought Bobo might dodge her again, but he let her lift him up.

"You knew me the day I was born?" he asked, seeming enchanted by the notion.

Obviously he didn't understand what it meant that this woman was our real mother.

"Don't you mean you haven't carried Bobo since he was *a few days* old?" I asked her. "The Freds always said Edwy and I were the only ones taken to Fredtown on the very day of our birth."

Was I trying to get her to speak of my birth just as wistfully as she did Bobo's? Was I trying to get her to solve the mystery of why Edwy's and my removal to Fredtown had been different from every other child's? Was I just showing off? I'm not sure. Everything in my head and heart was jumbled.

The woman gave me such a sharp glance, it felt like a knife cutting through the air.

"I only saw Bobo that first day," she said. "A Fred took him right from my arms. I don't know where the Freds took him the next day, or the day after that. My own child, and I knew nothing. The Freds were everywhere back then. People said they could sniff out a woman giving birth anywhere, no matter how she tried to hide."

The way she said "Fred" was like how someone back in Fredtown might say "poison" or "evil" or "villain" or "hate" when they were trying to make a story scary on purpose. When they were pretending there were bad things in the world.

Freds weren't bad. Freds were good.

I recoiled, and made a noise that might have been a whimper. I wanted to say, *No, no, you don't understand! The Freds only did that because they had to, because they wanted to keep us children safe.* . . . But the words stuck in my throat.

"What kind of a baby was I?" Bobo asked, as if that was all he cared about.

The woman nuzzled her face down into Bobo's curls, just like Fred-mama, Fred-daddy, and I myself had done a thousand times since Bobo was born. Or—since he'd arrived in Fredtown.

"Oh, Bobo, you were the sweetest little baby I'd ever seen," she said. She caught me watching and her cheeks flushed, as if she knew she was really supposed to say, *I mean, you and your sister were the two sweetest babies I'd ever seen. The two of you are both my favorites. Of course I can't choose between you.*

That's the kind of thing Fred-mama or Fred-daddy would have said. They would have corrected themselves instantly. They were as good at that "favorite" thing as Mrs. Osemwe, the Fredtown school principal.

This woman just narrowed her eyes at me and repeated, "Yes, Bobo, you were the sweetest baby ever."

Bobo's legs dangled awkwardly on either side of the woman's hips. Pure meanness crawled into me, and I wanted to say, *You don't even know how to carry a little kid, do you? You don't know how to be a mother at all. Because you haven't been one the past twelve years. Not for real.*

Was this what it felt like to be Edwy? To want nothing so much as to say and do bad things?

You don't want to hurt Bobo, I reminded myself. *You want him to stay good and sweet and innocent and unharmed more than you want this woman to know how mad you are.*

And . . . I still did want her to like me. I wanted her to see that she'd been wrong to act so mean. Wrong to try to slap me.

I pressed my lips together even harder. I imagined even a crowbar couldn't open them.

The woman started walking again, and I followed her. We got to the other side of the caged-in building, and a wide street lay before us. Other parents and children were piling into cars and funny little bicycle cabs; motor scooters wove through the crowd with as many as four or five people crowded onto the seat. I even saw one laughing couple clutching a baby and jumping onto a skateboard.

Nobody wore a helmet. Any Fred I knew would have been horrified. They would have said everything but the cars were unsafe. (And maybe the cars, too, if there weren't seat belts. Which nobody seemed to be using.)

But Bobo loved anything with wheels. His eyes glowed and he bounced up and down in the woman's arms.

"What do we get to ride in?" he asked eagerly.

The woman frowned and shot me another glance that might as well have come with words attached: *You keep your mouth shut, young lady. I don't want to hear anything out of you.*

"We live close by," she told Bobo. "We don't need to do anything but walk."

We kept going, dodging cars and scooters and bicycles. I started feeling glad that the woman was carrying Bobo, because then I didn't have to worry about him getting run over. There didn't seem to be traffic laws, or if there were, they were no more complicated than *Try not to get killed.*

This place was nothing like Fredtown. Fredtown was clean and orderly, simple but tidy. This place was a lovely fountain marred by a rust stain across the marble; it was a nice-enough house next door to one with a collapsed roof and vines growing out of the chimney; it was ice-cream wrappers and chewing gum and what might have even been dog droppings all along the cracked sidewalk.

This was supposed to be home?

CHAPTER NINE

The house we were going to wasn't close. The woman and I both wore ourselves out taking turns carrying Bobo before she finally stopped in front of a door and pulled out a key. The door and the wall it stood in looked like there should be no need for keys or locks—they looked like you should have been able to give the wood one good push and knock the whole shack over: all four shaky walls and the rusted tin roof too.

The Freds say any house can become a home when there's a loving family, I told myself. *The Freds say if you don't like your surroundings, it's your job to brighten them. Maybe I should volunteer to paint.*

I was a little afraid that pressing a paintbrush against those walls would knock them down.

The woman's key rattled in the lock. A voice from inside yelled, "What took you so long?"

I half expected the woman to say, *It's Rosi's fault. She was a coward and hid Bobo from me.*

But the woman winced. Her hand shook, and she had to stop for a minute from trying to turn the lock. I saw her swallow hard, and then she called back, "They're here. They're really here. Our children."

And then the lock clicked and the door swung open. The woman pushed Bobo toward a shadowy corner.

"Your son," the woman said.

After the sunshine outside, it took my eyes a moment to adjust to the dim light inside the house. A gray-haired man sat in a dark corner, his face hidden in the shadows. Bobo bumped into the man's knees, and the man wrapped his left arm around Bobo's shoulders and pulled him close.

"Well, don't expect me to give you any better of a hug than that," the man said gruffly. "I've only got one arm."

"I've got two," Bobo said, which was so Bobo. He sounded as casual as if they were just comparing the length or curliness of their hair. Something that didn't matter.

The man turned toward the light, hugging Bobo, and I saw that the shirtsleeve at the other side of the man's body hung empty.

I waited.

Back in Fredtown there'd been a girl, Leila, who was born with a misshapen foot. She'd had surgeries to fix it, and now she was one of the fastest runners of all the seven-year-olds. But all along the way, as she progressed through casts and crutches, braces and special boots, there were always meetings where all the children of Fredtown found out exactly what was happening to her, how the bones were being reset, how we could help her while she healed. I remember some of the other little girls being jealous of all the attention Leila got, and then there were meetings about that, too.

But we always heard the story behind her injuries, her recovery. We always knew the explanation. From the time she could talk, Leila herself could rattle off the exact words she'd been told: *When I was born, my foot was like a flower that hadn't bloomed yet. The bones were curled together. I just had to have the doctors help the bones straighten out. That's all.*

I thought this man—our father—would tell Bobo and me the story behind his missing arm. He was the adult; we were the kids. I thought he would want to head off any rude questions Bobo might ask.

But for a long time he did nothing but hold Bobo in that one-armed hug. When Bobo started to squirm, the man let go and started to trace his fingers across Bobo's face. It was like he was trying to learn Bobo's face, like he used his fingers to see.

Could it be that the man's eyes didn't work and he really *did* need to use his fingers to see?

And he wasn't going to explain that either?

Bobo giggled.

"That tickles," he said.

The man let his hand drop.

"He's got a good face, good hair," the man pronounced. "Where's the other one? The girl?"

He really couldn't see. Couldn't see me standing in the doorway.

"Here," I said. The Freds would have wanted me to say, *Here, Father,* or *Here, Daddy; Here, Papa; Here, Dad.* But I couldn't do that, any more than I could call the woman Mother, Mama, or Mom.

The woman shoved me forward. Then she pushed down on my shoulders.

"Kneel," she said. "You're too tall."

I wanted to tell her, *It's wrong for someone who's bigger and stronger and older to be mean like that to someone who's smaller and weaker and younger.* But I was taller than her, and maybe stronger, too. She was just older.

It was wrong for her to say, "You're too tall," like that was a defect.

I stumbled forward, bumping against the man's knees just like Bobo had.

"She's old enough to help you sell the apples," the woman said, and there was something conniving in her voice, almost like a little kid wheedling for a piece of candy. "She'd be able to watch and make sure nobody steals from you."

What was she talking about? Was the man totally blind? Could he not see at all?

What kind of people would steal from a blind man?

The woman kept pushing me down, forcing me to crouch before the man. He put his hand out and ran his fingers across my face just as he'd done with Bobo. He froze when his fingertips brushed against my nostrils.

"She's got *that* kind of nose?" he asked. "What color are her eyes?"

I opened my mouth to answer—or maybe to ask what was wrong with my nose—but the woman spoke first.

"Brown," she said quickly. "They're dark brown, almost black, just like yours."

My eyes aren't brown, but green. Like . . . well, like the woman's own.

The woman squeezed my shoulder warningly. I turned to look at her. She put a finger over her lips and shook her head fiercely, her scowl deepening.

I glanced at Bobo. It wouldn't have been surprising for him to chime in, "Oh, don't you know your colors yet? *I* do! See, *this* is what brown looks like, and *that* is what green looks like," pointing first to his eyes, then to mine.

Bobo was turned away from the rest of us. He was watching a spider make a little web between the wall and the leg of the man's chair. He didn't say anything.

The woman jerked me up and back, away from the man.

"It's almost time to eat," she said. "Rosi can help me make supper."

"Okay," I said, trying to sound cheerful and helpful and kind. Not puzzled and angry and sad, like I really felt. "Bobo's good at setting the table, so we can both help."

Bobo still didn't say anything. I suddenly realized that if Bobo was really that interested in the spider, he would have pointed it out to the rest of us. He would have turned around exclaiming, *Look! Look! How does that spider do that? Why can't I spin sticky web stuff out of* my *belly?* Instead, he was standing there motionless, except for his shoulders quivering every now and then.

Bobo was crying, and trying not to let anyone see.

I recast the way I'd heard him say "That tickles" when the man was feeling his face. I recast the giggle I'd heard. Bobo's moods could turn like that, a giggle twisting into tears in an instant.

I remembered that Bobo sometimes hated being tickled.

I was a terrible sister for not remembering sooner.

I put my hand on his shoulder.

"Come on, B," I said. "We'll work together."

But the man slashed his one arm through the air and slapped his hand against his leg.

"My son doing women's work?" he said. "Never!"

Bobo's shoulders shook harder.

"Women's work?" I asked. "Setting the table isn't women's work or men's work! Preparing meals is everyone's work!"

Bobo whirled around.

"Fred-daddy cooks for us all the time!" he said. "I want my Fred-daddy! I want my Fred-mama! I want to go home! My real home, I mean, in Fredtown!"

I'd thought the woman was scowling before. Now her face was like the sky before a thunderstorm. Terrifying.

"Punishment," the man said. "They must be punished. They have to learn—"

"You'll go to bed without supper," the woman said quickly. She yanked me backward. Because I still had one hand on Bobo's shoulder, I jerked him backward, too. He tipped against me.

"But—," I began.

"*Both* of you will go to bed without any supper," the woman said. "Now. In there."

She pointed to a break in the wall where a tiny room seemed to hide. A hanging cloth in the doorway separated it from the rest of the house.

But it's still light out, I wanted to say. *And we don't even have our bags delivered from the airport. We don't have any clothes to sleep in. And . . . we didn't do anything wrong.*

The Freds had taught us to stand up for ourselves when we were falsely accused. They'd taught us to explain away misunderstandings calmly and peacefully. They'd taught us everything about how to behave in Fredtown, with Freds.

But we weren't in Fredtown anymore. These adults weren't anything like Freds.

There was something bottled up in the woman's expression that really scared me. Rage, yes, but also fear. It was like she was a kid too. Like Bobo and me. Little kids were the ones who got scared and angry. Not adults. And who was she scared of and mad at? The man? Bobo and me?

"We are tired after our long trip," I said stiffly. Suddenly I just wanted to get away before I said or did anything awful. "Come on, Bobo. I'm sure we'll feel better after a good night's sleep."

"Not tired!" Bobo wailed. "Not sleepy! Not—"

I picked him up. He kicked at me like he was throwing a tantrum—something he probably hadn't done since he was two. I kept holding on, hoping it would calm both of us.

"Shh," I said, stroking Bobo's hair like Fred-mama always used to do. "Shh. It's okay. Everything's okay."

I carried Bobo into the tiny room, and it was a relief to be away from the woman's glare, the man's anger. I let the cloth drop behind me, hiding us. There was nothing in that little room except a lamp on an upturned orange crate and a thin blanket spread on the floor.

"Look how soft this blanket is," I said, leaning down to

pat it. "Look how nicely it's spread out, just waiting for you and me."

"Don't like that blanket!" Bobo cried. "Want *my* blanket! Want my bed! Want to go back to Fredtown! Want—"

"Shh," I whispered in his ear, as I eased him down onto the blanket. "Calm down. Would eating help? I've still got a bag of raisins and a peanut butter sandwich in my knapsack. . . ."

Was it wrong to offer him that when we'd been sent to bed without our supper? My Fred-parents had never used that as punishment, so I couldn't be sure.

It didn't matter, because Bobo screamed, "No! Not hungry!"

I understood. My stomach felt too achy and sad for me to even think about food. I couldn't believe I'd ever be hungry again.

But what if the man and the woman heard Bobo yelling and realized that we didn't care about supper, so they'd think of some *worse* punishment?

"Listen," I whispered again to Bobo. "You can tell me everything that's making you sad or mad. Sometimes that helps. You can tell me anything you want. But tell only me. Whisper. Don't let anyone else hear."

"Want my Fred-daddy," Bobo said, and while it wasn't a whisper yet, at least he wasn't screaming. "Want my Fred-mama. Want my toy sailboat."

"We packed that, remember?" I whispered in his ear. "It will probably be here by the time we wake up tomorrow."

"Want my monkey bars," Bobo said, and now this was more like a murmur.

"I bet there's a playground here, too," I said. "Maybe their monkey bars are even better."

"Want . . ." Bobo went on listing everything he missed about Fredtown. Every third or fourth word was "Fred-mama" or "Fred-daddy." Only when I was sure he was more asleep than not did I dare to let myself whisper back, "Oh, me, too, Bobo. I want our Fred-parents too."

Except that I knew the kind of thing they would say to me if they were here, even if they'd witnessed everything the man and woman had said and done. I could just hear Fred-daddy's voice in my head, telling me, *I think you just don't understand the reasons behind those things you were insulted and hurt by. You just don't understand your real parents. If you understand other people's viewpoint, you can think of them more kindly. And you can stop focusing on your own anger and pain.*

I did still want my Fred-mama and Fred-daddy. I wanted to go back to Fredtown as much as Bobo did.

But I also wanted something I thought might be possible, something I promised myself I would find a way to do tomorrow:

I wanted to talk to Edwy.

CHAPTER TEN

In the morning, when I woke up, the space on the blanket beside me was empty. I was confused for a moment—*Blanket? Floor? Where's my bed?*—but then my empty stomach twisted painfully and I remembered everything: Bobo and me being sent to bed without supper, the man who was supposed to be our father yelling that we had to be punished (*for what?*), the woman who was supposed to be our mother scowling and glaring at me, and telling me I babied Bobo.

Where *was* Bobo?

Back in Fredtown, he'd never wandered off in the night, and this new place—our new/old home—had to have scared him yesterday as much as it scared me. . . .

Just then I heard laughter on the other side of the wall: pure, clear laughter flowing like a river of joy.

It was Bobo.

Thinking about how his giggle the day before had been followed by tears, I scrambled to my feet. I was still wearing the dress I'd worn yesterday—and the entire time on the plane the night and day before that. My hair was probably sticking out in all directions, and I had no comb to tame it. But all I could think of was getting to Bobo.

I spun around the open edge of the wall, into the next room.

Bobo was sitting at the small, rickety table—sitting on the woman's lap, actually. He had a fork raised in the air and his head was tilted back, his curls resting against the woman's collarbone.

"Bobo!" I said, and somehow everything I was confused or worried about made his name come out sounding harsh. "Be careful! If you're eating and laughing at the same time, you might choke!"

"She said I could put sugar on my pancakes!" Bobo burbled. "Then . . ." He let out another fountain of laughter. "Then she said that for all she cared, today I could have sugar on my sugar, if I wanted it!"

The woman shot me a glance that just dared me to remind Bobo that eating too much sugar made him bounce off the walls. She hugged him closer.

I glanced toward the corner where the man had been sitting the night before.

"He went to the privy," the woman said.

"The father," Bobo said, as if he wasn't sure I'd understand.

I kind of liked how Bobo put it—"*the* father," not "my" or "our." I could do that much.

Bobo stabbed his fork into a mess of pancake pieces on the plate before him, but stopped before bringing it up to his mouth.

"Does the father feel people's faces every time he sees them?" Bobo asked.

The woman—the mother—glanced toward the back wall of the house and lowered her voice.

"He can't see," she said, her face pinched. "That's why he touches. He wasn't always like this. Just since—"

"Since what?" I asked.

The mother shook her head. Now the expression on her face was like a door slamming shut.

"There's hotcakes on the stove for you, too," she said, motioning with her head.

I walked to the stove. I wanted her to offer me sugar as well. I wanted her to say I could have sugar on top of sugar, just like Bobo. But she didn't.

The pancakes left in the skillet were shriveled and not even lukewarm. There was a fly crawling on the one plate laid out on the cracked counter beside the stove.

My Fred-parents would never expect me to eat off a fly-specked plate, I thought. *They would never give me the left-behind breakfast.*

But my brain was rebellious too, that morning. It shot back at me, *And if they were here now, they'd say, Rosi, Rosi, Rosi, aren't you capable of washing off your own plate? Aren't you capable of heating up your own food?*

I wished my Fred-parents were there to call me *Rosi, Rosi, Rosi.* I wished they were there even if they were gently scolding me. I washed off my plate in the sink and pretended I didn't notice the slight brown tinge to the water. But I slung a little hotcake onto my plate without bothering to turn the fire on under the skillet first. I had a feeling the food would stick in my throat no matter how cold or hot it was.

I sat down with Bobo and the mother. Bobo had his mouth full, and neither the mother nor I said anything for a moment. I worked out dates in my head: It was a Saturday or, at the latest, a Sunday. Not a school day.

"I could run errands for you today," I said. I felt devious. Back in Fredtown I could have just asked, *Can I go see my friends? Can I go talk to Edwy?* But here it felt like I had to hide what I really wanted. "If you need me to go to the store, I know how to barter for a good price. I won't forget to get the change when I pay."

The mother pressed her lips into a thin line.

"You'll help with the apples," she said. "This afternoon. This morning we'll go to church. You and me and Bobo. It's Sunday."

"Church?" I said, trying out the word, the idea.

"Didn't you ever go to church in . . . that place?" the mother asked. She meant Fredtown. I could tell. But she said "that place" like even those words hurt her mouth.

I looked at Bobo shoveling sugar-covered pancake pieces into his mouth. How much did he understand? How much of the tension in the mother's voice did he hear?

"We had religious studies in school," I said, trying my best to keep my tone even and unconcerned. "We learned the best tenets of all religions: *Be kind. Do unto others as you would have them do unto you. Cultivate right thought and right speech. Forgive those who trespass against you.*"

"All religions," the mother repeated. She sounded like she didn't believe me. "Didn't they tell you there are some false prophets who lead people into evil ways, not toward goodness and light? Or did they not even tell you about the evil ones?"

A noise came from behind the house—maybe a door slamming. Maybe it was the father leaving the privy.

The mother stood up, practically dumping Bobo from her lap. He landed on his feet and kept chewing.

"Hurry!" the mother said. "It's almost time to go." She looked me up and down. "Don't the two of you have any other clothes than that? You're wrinkled."

Did she think we'd carried everything we owned in

our knapsacks? Didn't she know about our luggage? Wasn't someone going to deliver it? Wasn't it a mother's job to keep track of her children's things?

"We have lots of other clothes," I said. "When are our suitcases coming from the airport?"

The mother narrowed her eyes at me.

"You didn't tell me you had suitcases," she said.

"I thought—"

The mother waved a dismissive hand, not waiting for me to straighten out my thoughts.

"You and your father can pick them up this afternoon," she said. "If they haven't been stolen."

Why did she sound like it would be my fault if someone stole our bags?

The back door of the house creaked open and then banged shut, making the walls shiver. The father stepped into the shadows just inside the door. It felt like he was watching us, even though he was only listening.

"You could come to church with us," the mother told him, her voice breaking. "We could be a complete family, giving thanks together. Everyone would see—"

"Humph." The father gave a grunt of disgust. It was a sour, bitter sound. "You know *I* can't see. You know I won't go there."

I looked back and forth at the mother and the father. If

they'd been my Fred-parents, they would have exchanged a glance, then Bobo and I would have been sent out to play, and when we returned all the tension between them would have been talked out and gone.

But these were my real parents. One of them was blind, and the other didn't seem to have any expressions on her face besides glaring and sorrow and anger and fear.

The mother began making shooing motions with her hands.

"Take your turn in the privy," she told me. "At least smooth down your hair. Then let's go. Hurry!"

Five minutes later—my hair semitamed, my dress no less wrinkled for my trying to straighten it out—the mother and Bobo and I stepped out the front door, leaving the father behind in his dark corner.

I wouldn't have said the mother was joyful walking to church, but there was a certain eagerness to her step that I hadn't seen before. Bobo skipped along beside her, bouncing up and down in a way that might have been because of all the sugar he'd had for breakfast, but might have happened anyway. Bobo was always a big skipper.

Doesn't he see how scary all the houses on our street are? I wondered. I was paying more attention than I had the day before. I could see that our house—ramshackle as it was— was actually one of the nicer ones in the neighborhood.

The others were mostly boxes and boards propped together randomly, spackled with dried mud. They looked like they could be knocked down by no more than the breath of a child making a wish blowing on dandelion fluff.

"This way," the mother said, tugging Bobo and me onto a dirt path winding through a field of weeds.

It wasn't long before we came to a large open building made of cinder blocks that stopped halfway up, with solid-looking posts leading the rest of the way to a shiny tin roof.

A crowd of some thirty-five or forty people had already gathered—maybe we were late. We took up a place at the back and sat down on the floor. I looked around at the other kids.

If Edwy's here, I thought, *then . . .*

Edwy wasn't there. But I did see Cana, the little girl he'd once had spy for him. A man who must have been her father had his arm around her shoulder, holding her close—maybe at least she had real parents who were nice. She shyly raised a hand and waved at me from across the room. I really wanted to see Aili, too, the girl the rude man had grabbed from me on the plane yesterday, but she was also missing. Most of the children around us were babies and toddlers.

Someone I couldn't see began blowing on a flute, and five adults stood up at the front and started singing about joy and rejoicing. Around us, people began to stand up and dance in place, waving their hands in the air, throwing their heads back and singing along.

"Can I dance too?" Bobo asked, leaning toward me.

"Yes," the mother said loudly, as if he'd been asking her, not me.

I nodded, because if Bobo was happy enough to dance, it would be wrong to hold him back. Both he and the mother stood up and joined hands and began swinging their arms and their hips back and forth in time to the music. But I sat still, because I wasn't happy. I didn't feel like dancing or singing about joy.

Finally the music ended and everyone sat down, even the singers. A man stepped up to a table in the front. Maybe it was an altar; it held nothing but a rough wooden cross.

So this is a Christian church, I thought, as if I expected my religious studies Fred-teacher to be proud of me for knowing that. *Christian, not Muslim or Buddhist or Hindu or Jewish or Taoist . . .*

The mother glanced over and must have seen me watching the man at the front.

"Pastor Dan is a missionary," she whispered. "That's why he looks so different. But don't . . . don't hold it against him. He's been so helpful. . . ."

Looks so different? I thought. The man had just bowed his head in a silent prayer—was that what the mother meant?

Another thought occurred to me, one that made me uncomfortable. Was she pointing out the fact that the man had paler skin than anybody I'd ever seen in person before? And that his eyes tilted in a way I'd seen only in pictures?

That was wrong to focus on, rude to talk about.

"What he looks like doesn't matter," I whispered back to the mother, just like the Freds would have wanted me to.

Something eased in the mother's expression.

"I just started coming here a month ago," she murmured. "So I'm still learning. But the things he says, the way he sees things . . ."

"Yes, the Freds always said it's the content of a person's character we should pay attention to, not how they look," I said. "That's what the Freds taught."

I thought she would be glad that I was agreeing with her, that the Freds agreed. But she flinched, and anger flashed across her face. Still, she didn't lash out, like she had before. She jerked her head forward and closed her eyes, as if she felt a sudden need to pray, too.

I didn't think I should try to say anything else to her, and it felt wrong even to notice all the ways this man looked different. So I thought about the word "missionary" instead. We'd talked about missionaries in religious studies class back in Fredtown: They were people who went to a foreign land to share their religion.

I remember Edwy asking all sorts of questions.

"Isn't that rude and disrespectful, to be a missionary?" he'd challenged the teacher. "Isn't that like saying to the people in the places they travel to, 'The religion you believe in now is totally wrong and mine is right'? Why is that allowed, if people are supposed to have respect for everyone who's different from them?"

The Fred-teacher had surprised us both by saying, "I cannot comment on that. In a sense, I myself and all the other Freds are missionaries. . . ."

Then I started asking questions too, but the Fred-teacher said that was the end of school for the day.

When we went back the next day, we had a different teacher.

The missionary at the front of this church finished praying, put his hands up in the air, and called out, "Praise be to God!"

"Praise the Lord!" all the adults around me shouted back at him.

"Isn't this the most glorious day?" the pale man asked. "You have your children back! For twelve years you wept for your children, just as Rachel wept for her children in the Bible. But now you have your children back! They were returned to you! You stood up against evil, and now, by the grace of God, you have triumphed. Your patience and persistence have been rewarded. The evildoers have been vanquished!"

His voice thundered in my ears, his words worming their way into my brain.

Stood up against evil . . . The evildoers have been vanquished. . . .

And then I understood: He was talking about the Freds. He was saying the Freds were evil.

I bolted upright; I was on my feet before I was conscious of deciding to stand.

"Stop it!" I screamed at the pale man. "Stop!"

CHAPTER ELEVEN

Everybody stared at me.

I'd wanted to say, *The Freds aren't evil! They're the kindest people ever. Take it back, what you just said!* I'd wanted to say, *Oh, right, while you're feeling so triumphant and gloating about your victory, did you ever think about what it feels like to be a kid ripped away from Fredtown? From our Fred-parents and everything we've ever known? Did you ever think how confused and scared we are? Did you ever think of just being kind and patient, and explaining everything? What if you're actually the ones doing evil? Did you ever think of that?*

But everyone was staring at me.

It wasn't like how everyone watched me when I was the narrator in the school play back in Fredtown. Then, every single gaze was kind and encouraging; every face seemed to be saying, *Oh, you're doing so well! I'm so happy to see you succeed! I'm rooting for you!*

The faces staring at me now in this cinder-block building

were all grim and disapproving. And I didn't have to guess at what the people around me were thinking, because I could hear them start to murmur:

"Who's *that*? Who does she think she is, interrupting like that?"

"Surely that's not one of the children, is it? She's so tall!"

"What if that's one of those Freds, who snuck back in, after all? She sounds like a Fred!"

I couldn't speak. I could barely breathe.

Bobo flung himself at my leg.

"This is my *sister*," he cried, grabbing on tight. "She's Rosi! She's not a Fred!"

Bless brave little Bobo. He gave me the courage to take a deep breath, and that helped. Everyone was still glaring at me, though, except for the missionary at the front, who mostly looked puzzled and concerned. So did the little kids who were old enough to be paying attention. My eyes met Cana's, and she mouthed something at me. Was it *Be careful*? Was she smart enough to know to say that?

Behind me, a baby started to cry.

"I—," I began. I choked on the word and had to try again. "I think you forgot how scared little kids can get, hearing about evil. And how much babies cry. If you want, I can take all the little kids out into the field to play until the service is over."

This was a cover-up, a replacement for what I was too scared to say.

Bobo nodded vigorously, his head bouncing up and down against my leg.

"You can take *me* out into the field to play!" he said, his voice so merry it was like he didn't notice anyone glaring at us. "Especially if there's going to be a lot of sitting still and listening. I'm not very good at that."

Any Fred would have laughed, and then gently told Bobo that the only way he was going to get good at sitting still and listening was by practicing sitting still and listening. But no one said anything in this cinder-block church.

The baby behind me cried louder. I glanced back, and the mother holding the baby didn't even seem to know she should bounce him up and down and murmur, "Shh, shh. You're okay." The mother just sat there, watching her baby cry.

The pale man at the front tilted his head sideways, watching me.

"It's true we are out of practice dealing with children, and thinking about what children need," he said. "Next week we'll have Sunday school classes and start taking turns with nursery care. But for this week, maybe it would be best if this girl—Rosi?—takes all the children out into the field to play until our service is over."

I reached back for the crying baby. The mother didn't

seem to know what to do except hand him over. The baby's fat little hand grabbed one of my fingers, and I let him guide it into his mouth, between his gums.

"He's teething," I said. "That's all."

The baby gnawed on my finger, biting down so hard that it hurt. But at least he stopped crying.

The mother looked angry, not grateful.

"Come on, then," I said to Bobo.

He and I went out into the open field, me carrying the baby, a trail of other little kids following us.

"Who wants to play Duck Duck Goose?" I asked.

"Me! Me! Me!" the children around me cried.

I started arranging them in a circle. Someone tugged on my skirt.

I looked down and saw Cana looking up at me.

"No one is to be called an enemy," she said solemnly. That was one of the principles we'd learned in Fredtown. It was part of a longer quote, which also included the words *All are your benefactors, and no one does you harm. You have no enemy except yourselves.* The Freds always said this when a kid treated someone unfairly, or when we refused to take someone else's feelings into account. It didn't mean anyone had literally said "You're my enemy"—who would do that? It was just a sign that we were pushing someone away, acting divisive.

When Freds quoted this principle, they always seemed particularly sad.

"I didn't do anything wrong!" I said frantically now, to Cana. "That man just kept talking about evil, and—"

Cana blinked up at me, her tiny features so innocent and sweet. And knowing.

Was she right? Had I just turned every adult at that church into an enemy?

I'd never had an enemy before. Unless you counted Edwy.

CHAPTER
TWELVE

Church ended, and the parents came out to claim their children from the field. I'd kept the kids entertained and reasonably quiet for more than an hour in a space where there was nothing to do but run and shout and pick weeds. We'd played Duck Duck Goose, London Bridge, Ring-Around-the-Rosie, and, when I ran out of other games, Hunt for the Prettiest Flower. But none of the adults said thank you. They just stared at me distrustfully and whispered when they thought I wasn't looking.

The Fred thing to do would be to calmly and politely say, "Excuse me. Is there a problem? Is there some issue you would like to discuss with me?"

I couldn't do it. Not when they'd already been whispering about me being a Fred only pretending to be a child. Not if they thought Freds were evil.

The mother and Bobo and I walked back to our house.

"Nelsi?" the mother called as we pushed the door open.

Was this the father's given name? How could I not know that about my own father?

I didn't know the mother's given name either. Why hadn't the Freds told us that basic information? Why hadn't they done that years ago?

Had the Freds thought, even up to the moment we stepped on the plane, that we'd really never need to know our parents' names, because we'd never meet them?

I didn't ask the mother about names now. No one answered her, and she began wringing her hands.

"Looks like he's already left to sell the apples," she said. She stepped quickly through the house to the kitchen, scanning the table and countertops. The dirty skillet still lay on the stove. The mother reached for a loaf of bread. "Here, Rosi, you take a sandwich for him and a sandwich for you. Hurry! When he doesn't get lunch . . ."

"You want me to take him lunch," I repeated. "Can you tell me where he is?"

The mother paused in the middle of slapping sandwiches together and frowned at me as if my question annoyed her. As if it were my fault I didn't know where the father might be selling apples.

That's not fair, I wanted to say. *How would I know?*

I kept my mouth shut. But I could feel my lips puckering together into a sulk.

"He's downtown, of course," the mother said. "Where we were yesterday . . ." She seemed to remember that we'd followed a convoluted path coming from where the plane landed. "Look. All you have to do is go to the end of our street, where there's the creek. Follow the creek until it bends like a hairpin. Then turn to the left. That'll take you to the market. Where your father sells his apples. The two of you can bring your luggage home when you're done."

"Can I go too?" Bobo asked, bouncing up and down.

I was pretty sure it was the word "creek" that caught his ear. Bobo liked anything to do with water.

The mother's frown deepened.

"No, no, Rosi has to hurry. You'll slow her down," she said. "And maybe you should take a nap. You're not too old for naps yet, are you?"

How could she not know if her own son still took naps?

"He takes them when he gets up early," I said. "Like he did today."

Bobo gave me the stink-eye, because he hated naps.

The mother yawned.

"I could use a nap myself," she said. "I'll lie down beside you, and as you're falling asleep, I'll tell you stories. . . ."

"About when I was a baby?" Bobo asked eagerly.

"Sure," the mother said to him. "Here," she said, handing me the sandwiches, now wrapped in a ragged cloth. "Bring the cloth back when you come home tonight. Now go!"

She actually pushed my arm to hurry me up. I stepped out the front door, into the baking sunlight.

Bobo gets cuddled and told stories and I'm pushed out the door, treated like a servant, I thought bitterly. *That's not fair either.*

But immediately it was like all the Freds I'd grown up with were talking in my head: *Big kids should never be resentful of little kids getting special privileges, because you were treated that way too when you were little. And remember that as you grow and get more responsibilities, you also get more freedom and more rights, more opportunity to make your own choices . . .*

"Right," I muttered under my breath. "I got so much choice about whether to leave Fredtown, whether to come here."

But the Fred voices in my head had shifted my perspective. It was good to be outside, not trapped in that dark hut being forced to take a nap. It was even good to be alone for now. Maybe I would run into other kids; maybe I could ask around and find out where Edwy lived.

It was easy to find the creek, easy to walk along it on a dirt path clearly beaten down by lots of other feet before mine. Because the creek was lined with soaring trees, it was cooler there than along the street of falling-down houses.

Maybe I should just think of everything here as an adventure, I told myself. *Maybe the mother and father aren't so bad. Maybe I'll get used to them. Maybe I'll stop missing all the Freds.*

Just thinking that made me have to blink back tears. So I was looking down and barely paying attention when I heard a voice call from lower on the creek bank, "Rosi?"

It was Edwy.

CHAPTER THIRTEEN

He was standing at the edge of the water and holding on to a branch he'd evidently broken off from one of the trees. No—it was a pole.

"Nice," I said. "You've only been here a day and already you've run away from your parents to go fishing. And goof off."

"They're *making* me fish, Rosi," Edwy said. "They said I can't come home until I catch enough fish for the whole family. Aunts and uncles and cousins and everything. They say the Freds spoiled us and we don't know how to work."

"Oh," I said.

The way I was thinking shifted again. The creek here was wide but shallow, not much more than a trickle. It would take him a long time to catch any fish, let alone enough to feed a lot of people.

I was supposed to be hurrying sandwiches to the father for lunch. Edwy and I hadn't been friends in more than a year. But I sat down on the bank of the creek anyway, right behind Edwy.

"Are your real parents . . . okay?" I asked him. "Are you okay with being here?"

Edwy flicked his pole, sending the worm and hook on the end of his line into deeper water.

"You know I didn't like Fredtown, anyhow," he said.

"That doesn't guarantee you'd like it here," I countered. "There could be *two* places you hate."

I almost said, *Maybe you'd hate every place! Maybe you're the one who's hateful. Did you ever think of that?*

But I wasn't exactly enjoying being here either.

"Nobody answers my questions here, any more than they did in Fredtown," Edwy complained.

"I know," I said, even though I hadn't actually dared to ask many questions. I was kind of impressed that Edwy had.

"And . . . making me fish?" Edwy added. "That's really to punish me. Because they said I had to stop asking questions, and I didn't."

That didn't surprise me. I watched Edwy pull his line closer.

"Something bad happened here," Edwy said. "I can tell. And that's what no one will talk about."

It was on the tip of my tongue to say, *Well, duh! For twelve years they kept telling us it was too dangerous for us to live with our own parents. Of course something bad happened!*

Instead I said, "The father—I mean, my real father—he's blind and he's missing one arm. And I know he wasn't always like that, because the mother said so. And he thinks there's something wrong with my nose."

I winced, because that was like asking Edwy to say, *There is something wrong with your nose! It's ugly! Your whole face is ugly!*

That was how Edwy talked back in Fredtown, before I started avoiding him. Sometimes the Freds heard him and had long, stern talks about what was and wasn't appropriate to say about other people. But most of the time Edwy waited to say things like that when none of the Freds were listening.

Edwy stared down into the water.

"I'm sorry," he whispered.

Had Edwy really just said that? Edwy?

Somehow that made it possible for me to inch toward the topics I really wanted to ask about.

"I . . . I found an official decree on the floor of the airplane," I said, carefully avoiding the issue of which row of seats I'd found it in. I really wanted to say, *I know you stole it! I know what you're like!* But I struggled to keep my voice calm and neutral. "The bottom part was torn, so I don't know what it said after the part about the men on the plane leaving right away so our parents have total control over . . . something.

Did you see that paper, that decree? Did you read any more of it than I did?"

I expected Edwy to protest, *What are you accusing me of? You're the one who saw the decree, not me! Did* you *steal it? Did goody-goody Rosi actually do something wrong?*

But he just shook his head and muttered, "No, it was torn when I saw it too. I didn't see the rest of it. I wish I had. I wish I knew . . ."

"Everything," I whispered.

Edwy nodded. Our eyes met, his only a shade darker than mine.

I'd never noticed before how much our eyes were alike.

"Also . . . , I saw what you carved into your seat on that airplane," I said.

Edwy's expression turned into a defensive glare.

"Nobody said that wasn't allowed!" he protested. It was almost comforting how much he sounded like the Edwy I'd known back in Fredtown, the one who was so good at coming up with excuses.

I resisted the urge to roll my eyes.

"I'm not going to *tattle*," I said. "I just wanted to know . . . What did you mean? 'Those people aren't real either'? Did your Fred-parents tell you—"

"You know I wouldn't trust anything a Fred told me," Edwy said. "I hate them! They're all frauds and liars and . . ."

I felt my face harden into a glare to match his. It was unbearable to hear him say such awful things about the Freds when I missed them so much. Especially after the people back at my mother's church had called the Freds evil. But Edwy's criticism was worse, because he'd actually known the Freds. Even when he misbehaved, even when he was rude on purpose, they had never been anything but kind.

"Never mind," Edwy said, his voice softening. He gazed off toward the other side of the creek. "Even you have to admit there was something wrong with those men on the plane. You had to have hated them as much as I did."

"I don't *hate* anyone," I said automatically. This would have been the Fred-approved response—we were only supposed to hate things like cruelty, and thistles and thorns. Not people. But I instantly regretted my words. Saying what the Freds wanted me to say usually just made Edwy mad. I winced again. "But I *kind of* agree. Those men on the plane were . . ."

"Terrible," Edwy finished for me. "And . . . hiding something. Fake."

Not real either, I thought. His words carved into the seat had been about the men on the plane, not our real parents. I felt disappointed somehow. As if I'd been counting on Edwy to explain everything. To solve all my problems.

"You thought scratching graffiti into an airplane seat and addressing it 'Hey, world' was going to change anything?" I asked. I sounded as bitter and complaining as Edwy ever did back in Fredtown.

He shrugged.

"I thought maybe someday *someone* might see it, some-one might decide to help us. . . ."

Maybe the Freds had been more successful raising Edwy than any of them thought. He actually sounded hopeful. Idealistic.

I wished I could still feel that way.

"Doesn't it seem like every adult we've ever known is hiding something?" I asked. "Because they're the adults and we're the kids. Because we're not old enough yet to be told everything. Because . . ."

It struck me that only Freds gave those reasons. The men on the plane had just seemed to regard us kids as too much bother.

And my parents? I wondered. *What are their reasons for . . . being like they are?*

"Yeah!" Edwy said, as if he liked my question. He kicked at a clump of mud half submerged in the water. "I thought everything would be different here."

"It is," I muttered.

"No, more different," Edwy said impatiently. "Like . . . have you noticed that there aren't any kids older than us here either?"

"We're the oldest kids there are," I said, annoyed that he would treat this like a big deal. "It was like that in Fredtown, too. Remember?" I had to stop myself from adding *Have you forgotten everything from before yesterday?*

Edwy shook his head impatiently, making his hair flop to the side.

"No, *listen*," he said, like he actually cared what I thought. "They took you and me to Fredtown the day we were born. Because they didn't think we were safe here, right? If they really cared about kids' safety, wouldn't they have also taken the kids who were a year older than us, and two years older than us, and three years older than us, and so on and so on, all at the same time they took us?"

I'd never thought of that before. Not once.

"My family had a big party last night," Edwy said. "To celebrate me coming home. And—all the other kids, too. And all these aunts and uncles came. My real mom and my real dad have, like, eight brothers and sisters apiece, and they all have kids, too, so it turns out I have, like, eleventy-billion cousins. It turns out I was related to half the kids in Fredtown!"

This almost made me giggle. This was so much what Edwy deserved.

"So you're the oldest cousin," I said. "Big surprise."

"No," Edwy said, shaking his head again, more emphatically than ever. "I *wasn't*. I had cousins there who were grown-ups—twenty-five, twenty-six, twenty-seven—and then I had two or three cousins apiece at every age below mine. But between me and the twenty-five-year-olds—nothing."

Maybe I'd been sitting in the shade too long. I suddenly felt like shivering.

"Okay," I said slowly. "Maybe that's just . . . a coincidence. Or something."

I didn't even sound like I believed myself. I sounded spooked.

"Have *you* seen any kids older than us here?" he asked.

I thought about the people I'd seen on my long walk from the plane to the parents' house. I thought about the people I'd seen at the cinder-block church that morning.

"No," I said. "I haven't."

Edwy turned to face me directly.

"It wouldn't be just a coincidence for no babies to be born in my ginormous family for thirteen years," he said. "Or in this entire town. Something happened. What was it? What happened to all the kids who were little kids when we were born?"

CHAPTER FOURTEEN

"**I don't know**," I told Edwy. "I don't know, but I'll try to find out."

Edwy kept his eyes on me.

"Good," he said fiercely.

Maybe we looked at each other too long. Maybe there was too much we weren't saying. But suddenly it was weird again between Edwy and me. I scrambled to my feet.

"I've got to go," I said. "I have to take a sandwich to the father and help him sell apples all afternoon. My family is making me work too."

"You never minded it when your Fred-parents made you work," Edwy said.

I couldn't explain why it was different here. I wasn't going to tell Edwy about how the mother made me work while she gave Bobo sugar and cuddled him on her lap. I wasn't going to tell him how that made me feel.

"I've got to go," I repeated. "I'll be in the market if you

want to find me later. And . . . I live on the street where lots of people's houses are just broken boxes."

Edwy laughed, but not in a funny way.

"Half the town is like that!" he said.

"I guess," I said.

I really had to get away from Edwy now. If I stayed any longer, I'd say too much. I'd say things no Fred would want me to say.

I pretended I really cared about hurrying lunch to the father. I almost ran down the path. But right before the creek curved, I looked back through the trees. I had a clear view of Edwy wading farther out into the creek, struggling against the current.

And for that moment, I almost felt like I understood Edwy.

I turned away and kept walking.

When I got to the part of the creek where it curved like a hairpin, I turned left, back toward the town. Almost immediately, I found myself on a street that might have been part of the marketplace. The first building I came to had a row of tables in front of it, and each table contained . . . well, were they parts of a car? Parts of some kind of machine? All of it looked vaguely mechanical, but also dirty and broken. Still, I spoke politely to the man sitting by the nearest table: "Good afternoon, sir."

He narrowed his eyes at me, but didn't respond.

Didn't he hear me? I wondered. *Should I speak again more loudly? What if his ears don't work, the same way that the father's eyes don't work?*

But he was looking right at me. Even if he hadn't heard my words, he would have seen my lips move.

Could he possibly be both deaf and blind?

It seemed like he had both heard and seen me. It seemed like his narrowed eyes were his reply.

He's never seen me before in my life! I thought. *Why would he glare at me like that?*

A small child came racing out of the house behind him. It was Meki, one of the toddler twins who'd lived next door to me back in Fredtown.

"Wo-si!" Meki cried delightedly, running toward me.

The man intercepted her.

"Get back in the house," he growled, shoving her behind him.

"But—Wo-si! Love Wo-si!" Meki began to wail and struggle against his grip.

The man glared harder at me.

"Get away from here," he said. "Get off my property."

My knees began to tremble.

"Meki—I'll see you later," I said quickly, in a voice that also trembled. "Remember, you need to obey your . . . your father."

I forced my legs to move. I forced myself to walk away from Meki's sobs.

All she was going to do was run out and give me a hug! I thought, thoroughly puzzled. *Why wouldn't he want her to hug me?*

I remembered the grown-ups' glares at the church service that morning. I remembered the way the father had said, after feeling my face, *She's got* that *kind of nose?* I remembered the mother lying about what color eyes I have.

Is there something wrong with how I look? I wondered. *Something that nobody ever noticed back in Fredtown?*

Back in Fredtown, the Freds always said that it didn't matter how anyone looked. What mattered was what you did, how you behaved, how you treated other people.

But I just nodded abruptly to the next several people I passed. They were all adults, and I didn't trust my voice to try out greetings with them. Some of the people glared back at me; some moved their heads in a way that might have been a return greeting.

After the sixth or seventh person, I realized that all the people with brown eyes glared at me but all the people with green eyes nodded, even if it was the barest movement possible.

I'm not supposed to care if someone has green or brown eyes! I told myself. *Or any other color!*

I didn't think I'd seen anyone with any different eye color—though maybe the missionary at my mother's church had eyes that were more solidly black. . . .

Stop noticing eyes! I commanded myself. *Look for . . . look for whether or not you see anyone older than twelve but younger than twenty-five. Remember? You promised Edwy you'd find out about the people in that age group. What if it turns out that he's wrong and there are people that age all over the place?*

I didn't know how you could tell if someone was twenty-three or twenty-four rather than twenty-five. I'd never seen anyone who was older than twelve but younger than twenty. Back in Fredtown even the youngest teacher had been in his twenties. Almost all the Freds had been either parents or grandparents. The older Fred-parents—like mine—tended to be a little thicker around the middle than the younger ones; the Fred-grandparents were mostly gray-haired but still spry enough to chase after toddler grandchildren.

Not that I was supposed to be categorizing people based on their appearance. The Fred-grandparents were patient and kind and wise; the Fred-parents were too, but they were busier, and they were only patient up to the point when they would insist, "Yes, but regardless, it's time for you to go to school," or "Yes, we can do that later, after we all work together to fix dinner. . . ."

I could hear my Fred-parents' voices in my head speaking those words—those and all the other lines they used to gently redirect Bobo and me to what we were supposed to be doing, rather than what we wanted to do.

I was in danger again of making myself cry. It was too hard to think of my Fred-parents while people were glaring at me.

Stop looking at the people! I told myself. *Look at . . . the buildings! The streetscape!*

This was also different from anything in Fredtown. I was on a sidewalk now, but it buckled, as if the ground itself had heaved upward and was fighting against the concrete. I kept tripping, usually when someone glared at me. (*No, no—stop noticing!*) No one could safely run here, not without risking a face-plant with every other step.

The sidewalk and the street also meandered—off to the right, to avoid a pipe spewing greenish water (*Don't think about the germs and contaminants that might be in that water! Just don't step in it!*); then to the left, to dodge around a spot where the bricks and tiles from a broken-down house spilled out into the street. I missed the grid system and perfect right angles and tidy buildings of Fredtown all the more. In Fredtown you could always tell which direction you were going—north or south or east or west. Here, because the sun was precisely overhead, beating down on my neck and face,

I couldn't even guess which direction the street was turning, which way I was walking, where I was going.

That bothered me more than I ever would have guessed.

Eventually the street opened up into an area where the buildings on one side stood far apart from those on the other. I might have called it a square or a plaza if the boundaries hadn't been so uneven, if I'd been able to see the area as a whole. But everyone was crowded in so tightly that I could barely see past the backs and heads of the people around me. I was trapped between the brown tunic of a large woman in front of me and the hurrying legs of a man behind me. I caught a glimpse of piled scarves to my right and piled oranges to my left.

This was the marketplace. It had to be.

I let the crowd carry me forward. I held the cloth-wrapped sandwiches higher so they wouldn't be crushed. The people around me shoved and elbowed their way forward without even once saying *Excuse me* or *I'm so sorry—did I step on your toes?* I was glad I hadn't brought Bobo with me, glad I wasn't responsible for keeping him from being trampled or smashed between taller adults. (*Though what if I myself got crushed or trampled?*) I kept an eye out for apples and the father. But I ended up circling the marketplace three times before I saw him. He was off to the side, sitting with his back against a wall. His sightless eyes squinted fiercely at the crowd. He kept his one hand atop a pyramid of apples.

I didn't know how long he'd been sitting there, but it looked like he hadn't sold a single apple.

He can't see, I reminded myself. *He probably doesn't even realize that his squint looks mean and scares people away. He probably doesn't know that he's too far away from the crowd of shoppers.*

I made myself walk over to him.

"There's a space over there you could move to," I told him, pointing. Then I remembered that he couldn't see, and I dropped my arm. "Over there, more people would see your apples and you could sell them more quickly—"

"I have to lean against the wall," he growled at me. "It keeps my back from hurting so bad."

On top of everything else, he had problems with his back?

"I—I brought you a sandwich," I stammered, as if that were a way to apologize. "She—the mother—she made it for you."

The father grunted, twisted his face into an even uglier expression, and held out his hand. As soon as I placed a sandwich in his hand, he put his hand back on the top apple. Rather than bringing his hand to his mouth so he could eat, he leaned his head down to the sandwich.

Saliva from his mouth dripped down onto the apples.

"I—I'll watch the apples for you while you eat," I said. I forced myself to sit down beside him. "You don't have to worry about anybody stealing from you while I'm here."

"I always have to worry about people stealing from me," he muttered back to me. A few half-chewed crumbs from his mouth spewed out onto the apples. "What could you do to fight off thieves? You're a girl."

What did that have to do with anything?

I wanted to say, *What could you do? You're blind.* But that was evil and wrong and mean.

"I could scream for help," I said. "I could yell for the police."

The father snorted.

"Who'd help someone like you?" he asked. He waved the sandwich like he was scolding me. "Who'd help *us*?"

It almost made me happy that he used the word "us." Maybe he just needed to be cheered up; maybe he just needed to learn to trust people.

I didn't answer his question. Not directly.

"Is that sandwich good?" I asked. "The mother made one for me, too, but I'm not very hungry. You can have it too, if you want."

The father grimaced, as if my question had made the sandwich taste bad.

"Don't bother acting all goody-goody like that," he said. "You'll learn. Around here, you take what food you can get."

That sealed it. Now I really wasn't hungry. I searched for

something else to say, something that wouldn't make him snort or grunt or grimace.

I finally settled on "I think the mother was really sorry she didn't have a chance to make you your noonday meal before you left for the market. I think she really wanted to make sure she took good care of you."

This was another failure: The father snorted in an even more disgusted way than before.

"She shouldn't have gone to that church, then," he said. "She shouldn't go anyway. She should know those aren't our people. That man . . ."

"The leader?" I said. "The . . . missionary?"

"Yes," the father said. He looked angrier than ever. Could I count it as a minor victory that now he seemed to be more disgusted by someone else than he was by me? "She knows that man is an outsider. A *nakca*."

"What's a *nakca*?" I asked. I was pretty sure I'd never heard the word before.

"A foreigner," the father said. His face twisted in disgust. No—maybe it was hate. "Someone who comes in and tries to change things to the way he wants them to be. Even though he doesn't understand anything about real life. Or about us."

Somehow I didn't think I was part of this "us." I knew it for sure when the father added, "Like those Freds. The Freds were *nakcas*. The worst *nakcas* ever. And they turned my own daughter into a *nakca*, too."

I felt my face get hot. I was glad the father couldn't see me blush. I thought about how I'd suggested he move to a better place to sell apples.

But you could *sell more apples the way I suggested!* I wanted to protest.

Instead I said, "But I *want* to understand! I want to understand everything. If you explain, maybe I can."

The father turned his face toward me. His eyes stayed blank and sightless. I was, at best, nothing but a shadow to him.

"It's too late," he said. "It's hopeless."

And then he stopped talking.

CHAPTER
FIFTEEN

The father didn't speak to me for the rest of the afternoon. Between his silence and the way other adults looked past me, I almost felt like I had stopped existing.

I wasn't used to feeling invisible. In Fredtown, I'd been Rosi, the Oldest Girl, the one who always had to be responsible and set a good example. Everybody watched me. After Edwy and I stopped being friends, it wasn't like any of the Freds told the younger children, *Stop paying attention to Edwy! Stop looking to him as a role model! Rosi's the one you want to be like!* But . . . they might as well have.

Finally I saw some other kids in the marketplace walking alongside parents or being carried in grown-ups' arms. I started waving and calling to them, "Hello! How are you? Are you happy to be home?"

The first time I did that, to a seven-year-old named Lita, the woman with Lita grabbed her hand and yanked her to the other side, away from me.

The second time, it was a three-year-old named Oscar, and the woman carrying him pressed his face against her shoulder and kept her hand over his exposed ear, as if to make sure he couldn't see or hear me.

The third time, four-year-old Sano turned his head to smile shyly at me, and the man walking beside him gave Sano a . . . it was only a shove, wasn't it? Just to keep Sano going in the right direction? No adult would actually *smack* a child's rear, intending to cause pain.

Right?

Whatever it was—shove, smack, accidental push—Sano didn't seem to be expecting it. He pitched forward and slid across the cracked sidewalk. Then he started screaming. I stood up to help, but a woman scooped him into her arms before I could take the first step. I saw red on Sano's knees, and I opened my mouth, ready to warn the woman, *He's bleeding. He scraped his knees, and—*

The woman had already whirled around, clutching Sano's body tightly against her chest, as if she thought I wanted to steal him.

"This is your fault," she hissed.

Sano kept screaming. But I shut my mouth. I sat back down.

That woman had dark eyes, I thought. *Like all the other adults who glared at me. Did Lita's and Oscar's parents have brown eyes too? Should I check out grown-ups' eye color before I speak to any more kids?*

I couldn't do that. It went against everything I'd ever been taught. I couldn't refuse to speak to kids I'd known their entire lives—kids who were my friends, kids I liked and maybe even loved—just because they were with adults with brown eyes.

I decided I'd have to settle for just nodding at everyone.

Strangely, very few of the other kids did much more than that themselves. Fredtown had been such a friendly place—it was a rare morning when I made it all the way to school without some little kid running up and giving me a sticky-fingered hug. Fred-mama used to tease that for such a neat, tidy child, it was ridiculous how often I came home with muddy handprints around the collar of my dress (from Peki, little Meki's twin brother, who loved playing in the dirt) or chocolaty handprints around my waist (from when the kindergartners were doing a baking unit).

But here the other children mostly returned my nods with furtive glances and secretive nods back—it seemed like an extreme act of daring when eight-year-old Oram raised an eyebrow at me and tilted up the corners of his mouth the slightest bit.

Were they just imitating me, taking their cues from how I behaved? Or was something else at work?

I thought about the man's hand slamming against Sano's

rear. I thought about the mother—*my* mother—almost slapping me yesterday. I thought about how Bobo and I had been sent to bed without supper. I thought about Edwy being forced to fish for asking too many questions.

How many other kids had been punished for doing things we'd all considered perfectly normal in Fredtown? How many other kids had been treated differently by green- or brown-eyed adults? How many other kids were just as puzzled as I was, and had decided just to watch and listen until they figured everything out?

That's just what the Freds taught us to do, I thought. After all, one of our principles was *You learn something every day if you pay attention.*

I stared out into the crowd and looked for details I hadn't noticed before.

I saw a man selling pears in bags and hiding half-rotten ones under the shiny, beautiful ones at the top of the bag.

I saw a woman brush against another woman's arm and they both jerked back as though they'd touched poison. Each turned to yell at the other, so I could tell: One had green eyes; one had brown.

I saw a man scuttling along the ground like a crab. No— he was on a flat board balanced on three wheels. Then, as he passed, I saw why: He had no legs. He was missing even more limbs than the father.

Sometimes that happens, I told myself, remembering lessons in science class. *Like Leila, the girl born with a twisted foot, sometimes people are born with different bodies than others.*

Then I saw a man missing both arms.

A woman missing an arm and a leg.

A man with scars across his face that totally hid his nose.

That had to be from an injury. Nobody would have been born like that. Somehow, I was certain.

Why weren't any of the Freds like that? I wondered. *When so many adults here are . . . damaged?*

I touched my own face; I looked down at my own arms and legs, all so sturdy and brown and useful. I thought about how Edwy and I had agreed that something bad had happened here—something that had made the people who were kids when we were born disappear; something that had made the Freds take away the two of us and all the other children born after us for twelve solid years.

Something that had left so many, many adults scarred and damaged.

Something bad had happened, yes. I'd known that. But back in Fredtown, when the Freds talked about keeping us safe, I'd never imagined anything this bad.

What if the "something bad" happened again?

CHAPTER SIXTEEN

"I need to go check on Bobo," I told the father as I scrambled to my feet.

He jerked his head toward me, toward the sound of my voice. Maybe he hadn't been shunning me. Maybe he'd only fallen asleep, and since he was blind, he did it with his eyes open.

"What?" he said. "What are you talking about?"

"Bobo," I repeated. "I need to go make sure he's okay."

"He's okay," the father said, grunting again. "He's with his mother. That's where he should be."

"You don't understand," I said. There was an urgency growing in me I couldn't explain. It was like I had a physical need to see Bobo just then—I needed that more than I needed the sandwich I still hadn't eaten. "I have to see him. I have to be sure he's all right."

I was thinking of Bobo's arms and legs, the way they were so cute and little-boy pudgy. He hadn't lost his baby fat yet.

But he was so strong—I thought about him racing me to the playground in Fredtown; I thought about him jumping up and down on my bed after we found out we were coming home.

"Bobo has to be safe," I told the father.

Maybe blind people can hear extra things to make up for not being able to see. The father tilted his head, listening to me.

"What did you just see?" he asked.

"Hurt people," I said. "People without arms and legs, people with scars . . ."

"Old wounds?" the father asked. "Or new ones? Did you see any blood?"

He turned his head from side to side, as if he were trying to see too, or letting his ears scoop up as many sounds and voices as possible.

"I saw a little boy fall and scrape his knees," I said. "All the other wounds were old. I think."

The father sagged against the wall behind him.

"You scared me," he said.

I wasn't comforted.

"Please," I said. "Let me just—"

"Fine," the father said, biting off the word. "We'll stop for the day. I haven't sold any apples anyhow. Today's no different from any other day."

He stood up and began piling apples into a bag I saw he'd been sitting on for the past several hours. I reached out and held it open for him. I was still worried about Bobo, but something clicked in my head.

"You never sell any apples?" I asked.

"Not often," he muttered, still placing apples in the bag.

I thought about how, back in Fredtown, Edwy and I had learned about running a business—and learned that business owners have to sell enough to make a profit. I thought about our Fred-parents explaining that they had to work to support our family.

"But if you don't sell very many apples, then how do you . . . ," I began.

"Make any money?" the father finished for me. He made a disgusted sound deep in his throat. "Afraid you've come home just to starve? Don't worry, girlie. That's what the Victims' Assistance is for. They give us food and the other things we need. Like these apples I sell. They keep us just alive enough to stay miserable."

I knew what assistance was—it was help. Aid. One person giving something to another. But I'd never heard the word "victim" before.

"What's a victim?" I asked.

The father put the last apple in his bag.

"People like me," he said.

People missing arms or legs, I thought. *People who are blind or deaf. People with scars or paralyzed faces.*

The father made that disgusted, angry sound again in his throat as he heaved the bag of apples over his back.

"Everyone here," he said. "All of us."

Why did it seem like he thought I was in this "us" too?

The father started to walk away from me. For a moment I could only watch his lurching stride, the way he seemed to know to avoid people in his path. And the way people dodged him.

Then I scrambled to catch up.

"Are there victims who *aren't* here?" I asked. "People who left because . . ."

Because of whatever bad thing happened twelve years ago, I thought. *Whatever took away all the people who were kids when I was born.*

I was working on a theory—a cheerful one, even. Maybe Edwy had gotten me all scared and worried for nothing. Maybe when we were taken to Fredtown, and raised by Fred-parents, the older kids were taken to a . . . a Tedtown or a Nedtown or a Frederica-town, or something like that. Maybe they just hadn't come back yet. Maybe it was like we were part of a scientific experiment, and they were the control group.

I didn't really want to be part of a scientific experiment,

but it didn't *have* to be that something truly awful had happened to those kids.

I looked to the father weaving his way through the crowd, and I saw instantly that my question was a mistake. It turned his face to stone.

"I told you I wasn't going to explain," he said. His voice was hard too. "We're going home to check on Bobo. Isn't that enough for you?"

I couldn't speak. It wasn't enough. But I nodded anyway, forgetting that he couldn't see.

CHAPTER SEVENTEEN

"**Where are** the suitcases?" the mother asked as soon as we pushed our way in the front door.

"Bobo?" I called, ignoring her question.

She grabbed my shoulders as I walked by.

"I finally got him to go to sleep," she said, jerking me back. "Don't wake him up!"

I struggled against her grip. It took me only a second to break away.

"I just have to see him," I said in a slightly softer voice. But I darted past her, toward the room Bobo and I had shared the night before.

I reached the doorway before the mother could stop me. I stood there, gazing in, breathing hard.

Bobo was on the bare floor, sprawled flat on his back, his toes peeking out from under the blanket. He had the back of one hand resting on his forehead—Fred-mama used to joke that Bobo always slept in positions that made it look like he was about to recite Shakespeare. But he had his other hand against his mouth, his thumb on his bottom lip, the tip of the thumb braced against his upper teeth.

Bobo had pretty much stopped sucking his thumb when he was three. I could remember Fred-daddy explaining this to me: how kids sucked thumbs to comfort themselves, and gradually they realized they didn't need that comfort, or they discovered more mature ways to find it.

Bobo sucking his thumb again was a bad sign.

It wasn't just the safety of his arms and legs I needed to worry about.

The mother yanked me backward.

"Answer me when I speak to you," she demanded, standing practically nose to nose. "What happened to the suitcases you were going to pick up?"

Our suitcases. This morning they had been a huge concern for me. I'd wanted clothes to change into, a comb to unsnarl my hair, Bobo's toy boat to keep him happy. I'd wanted every bit of Fredtown those suitcases represented. But in my rush to check on Bobo, I'd completely forgotten about them.

"What suitcases?" the father growled.

"Didn't you tell him?" the mother asked, scowling at me. She turned to the father. "You and Rosi were supposed to pick up the suitcases she and Bobo brought from . . . you know. They were still at the airport."

"I forgot," I said. Our Fred-parents always wanted us to own up to our mistakes, but somehow that was easier back in Fredtown. Probably because our Fred-parents never glared at us so furiously. "I'm sorry. I was thinking about . . . other things."

I couldn't tell her how worried I'd been about Bobo. Not without sounding like I didn't trust her to take care of him.

"She looks like a grown-up, but she acts like an idiot child," the mother told the father, her voice mocking and angry. "Why, if *we'd* raised her, she'd know to use her head. She'd remember the things we told her."

I wasn't used to being talked about as if I weren't even there.

I wasn't used to being called ugly names. "Idiot" wasn't just worse than "dumb"; it felt a thousand times worse.

"I know it's my fault," I said, hanging my head. "Just tell me where to go at the airport and I'll get both suitcases, all by myself."

I thought that was a good offer—I was being Rosi the Responsible again, just like back in Fredtown. But both the mother and the father recoiled.

"You can't go out by yourself *now*," the mother said. "It's almost dark."

"I doubt those suitcases are still there, anyhow," the father said heavily. He sank into the chair I'd seen him in the night before. Then he turned toward the mother. "You know anything that isn't nailed down gets stolen. Why didn't you bring them home yesterday when you got the children?"

"*She* didn't tell me they had suitcases," the mother said. "How was I to know?"

I flinched.

"And I didn't know they wouldn't just be brought to our house," I said. My voice sounded weak and pleading. "That's how things would have been done in Fredtown. That's how things *were* done when we went to the airport there. A truck came around and picked up everyone's luggage, so no one had to carry it. I'd never been anywhere before but Fredtown. I didn't know anything would be different here—"

"Don't talk to us about that Fredtown!" the mother screamed.

I saw her swing her hand back. I saw it coming toward me. But I didn't move this time.

She'll stop herself, I thought. *She wouldn't ever really hit me. No adult does that.*

The palm of the mother's hand slammed against my face. She'd slapped me. The mother—no, *my* mother—had slapped me.

From inside Bobo's room I heard a cry.

"Rosi?" he called out. "Fred-mama?"

I saw the mother's face stiffen—outrage hardening over fury.

"I'm right here," I called to Bobo. I tried to keep my voice soothing and calm, even as my check throbbed.

Bobo pushed his way past the hanging cloth in the doorway of our room. His eyelids drooped sleepily and his curls stuck out at odd angles. One of the curls was plastered to his cheek.

"I had a nightmare," he whispered. He blinked at the mother and father. "Oh."

Was his nightmare that we'd left Fredtown and our Fred-parents, and come here? Was it that the home we'd talked about and longed for our entire lives had turned out to be a terrible place? A place where people were broken and damaged and scarred, and his real mother could slap his sister— and might even slap him sometime too?

"Nightmares aren't real," I told Bobo. I made my voice firm and convincing, to be a guarantee against the creepiest dream. "Remember how . . ." I wanted to say: *Remember how Fred-mama and Fred-daddy told you that all the time?* But the mother had slapped me just for talking about Fredtown. I didn't want her to slap me in front of Bobo.

I settled for, "Remember how many times I've told you that?"

"You told me that," Bobo parroted.

He really wasn't awake yet. He probably hadn't heard the mother arguing with me.

He probably hadn't heard her slap me.

She slapped me! echoed in my head. *She really, truly, actually slapped me!*

I was numb. But I had to think about Bobo. I had to think about protecting him now more than ever.

I crouched down in front of him.

"Nightmares aren't real," I said again. "Here you are with your real mother and your real father—and me—and everything's fine. . . ."

I dared to glance up toward the mother. Her face was like a storm cloud, but she didn't say or do anything.

She wouldn't hit Bobo, I told myself. *She loves him more than she loves me, so she'd never hit him.*

But what could I do if she did?

CHAPTER
EIGHTEEN

Late that night a knock came at our door. We'd already eaten supper—a stiff, awkward event I was even less hungry for than lunch. I hadn't complained about being forced to help with preparation and cleanup while Bobo was allowed to play. Now he was pretending a stick was a motorcar, and zooming it all around the floor. I sat in a corner with the book Fred-mama had given me to read on the plane. But I wasn't reading that book even now. I was thinking hot, angry thoughts: *If the mother asks me where this book came from, I'm just going to come out and tell her. And I'm going to tell her she has no right to blame me—or Bobo—for having good memories of Fredtown. It's not our fault where we grew up. It's not our fault we were taken there or brought here . . .*

I wasn't used to having hot, angry thoughts in my head. I didn't know what to do with them. So that knock at the door was a good distraction.

That's what I thought, anyway. The mother and father

stiffened, and the mother clutched the father's shoulder.

"Nobody comes visiting this late at night," the mother said.

She's scared, I thought, hearing her voice tremble. *She's scared of a* knock.

I didn't want Bobo to hear her fear—or to be exposed to whatever she was afraid of—so I called softly, "Hey, Bobo, drive your twig-car over here and we'll make a ramp for it to jump over."

I was behind the table. It was the farthest I could get from the mother and father and still be in the house with them. It was also the farthest corner from the door.

But Bobo was already scrambling up joyfully, racing to the door, just like he always did anytime our bell rang back in Fredtown.

"Whooo is it?" he called. "Which friend has come to play?"

I saw the mother and the father both jump up, ready to stop him. But Bobo was clever with latches. He already had it unhooked and was pulling the door toward him.

Edwy stood in the darkness on the other side of the door. And . . . he had our suitcases with him.

"Edwy!" Bobo exclaimed, an expression like sunshine bursting over his face. Bobo had always loved Edwy.

The mother and the father sprang up and stood on either side of Bobo. The mother even put her hand on Bobo's shoulder and angled her body ahead of his, sending a clear message: *Bobo is ours! Stay away from him!*

"I brought the suitcases for you and Rosi," Edwy told Bobo.

"Who are your people, boy?" the father growled. "And why did *you* have Rosi's and Bobo's suitcases?"

Edwy's eyes darted to the side.

He's going to lie, I thought. Edwy and I may have avoided each other for an entire year, but I still knew him really well.

"I just saw nobody had picked these up yet," he said, shrugging. "I thought I'd do Rosi and Bobo a favor."

"Humph," the father grunted. As if he didn't believe Edwy any more than I did. "And your people? Who are your parents?"

Edwy has green eyes, like me, I thought. The mother did too, so maybe it was only kids with green eyes that the father didn't like. Maybe the father had learned about genetics in school, like Edwy and I had, and he was asking about Edwy's parents to figure out more about Edwy.

Even thinking that seemed crazy, but I stood up and started inching toward the door. It felt like I might need to protect Bobo again.

Or maybe Edwy.

"I can't say I've actually heard my parents speak their names," Edwy said, laughing the same way he always did in class back in Fredtown when he hadn't done his homework. "They told me to call them Mother and Father."

I saw the mother elbow the father over Bobo's head.

"Then what's your last name?" the father growled.

"I know!" Bobo burst out. "It's Watanaboneset! This is Edwy Watanaboneset! I remember, because Edwy makes a funny about how it should be 'Want-a-your-bone-set-if-you-mess-with-me?'"

I'd never heard Edwy make that "funny." It must have been something he started in the past year. I couldn't believe he'd said that around a little kid like Bobo.

I was close enough to the door now to see the mother's face go dark.

"He's a Watanaboneset," she muttered.

"That pack of thieves," the father agreed, scowling just as bitterly.

Don't talk like that in front of Bobo! I wanted to scream. And, *Edwy never even met his parents until yesterday! How can you be mad at him because of who his parents are?*

"Thank you for bringing our suitcases," I said instead, stepping up behind Bobo. "That was a nice thing to do. You even figured out where we lived."

Edwy's eyes met mine.

"You know I'm good at finding things out," he said. His words seemed to carry more weight than their actual meaning. He tilted his head, and I thought maybe that was supposed to be some sort of secret signal meant only for me. Maybe he'd found out something he couldn't talk about in front of the parents and Bobo.

Or maybe I was just imagining that. I wasn't much good at reading secret messages in people's eyes. Back in Fredtown, we hadn't needed them.

The mother looked back and forth between me and Edwy.

"Okay," she said. "We have the suitcases now. Hand them in. And then you can leave. It's too late at night for *honest* people to be out and about. Or standing in doorways, talking."

"Fine," Edwy said, shrugging again, as if he didn't even notice that she had insulted him.

He shoved the suitcases in through the doorway, and the mother shut the door on him so quickly, she almost smashed his fingers.

"My toys! Thanks, Edwy!" Bobo said, falling upon his suitcase and knocking it to the floor. He began struggling with the zipper.

I could barely watch, because the mother and the father turned on me.

"Don't ever speak to that boy again," the mother said. "Stay away from him."

"He comes from a bad family," the father said. "A very bad family."

"He's my friend!" I protested, even though I wouldn't have used that word to describe Edwy back in Fredtown. "He brought us our suitcases!"

"His family probably stole them," the mother said, scowling harder. "They steal everything. They probably took all the valuables out, and then he just brought you what they didn't want."

I looked down at Bobo, who had his suitcase open on the floor and was already cradling his toy boat in his arms.

"Bobo, are all the toys you packed in there?" I asked.

"Sure," Bobo said. He didn't bother looking. I knew Bobo: As long as he had his hands on the toy he wanted at that particular moment, he could have a hundred others waiting to be played with, or none at all, and he'd be equally happy.

"Bah, toys," the father said. "It's clothes people steal. Clothes and jewels and . . ."

The mother reached for my suitcase.

I don't know what made me stop her. Nothing in my life in Fredtown had made me good at being secretive. I'd never wanted to hide anything from my Fred-parents. But suddenly I couldn't bear the thought of the mother touching the clothes Fred-mama and I had folded together.

"Look, I'll go put my things away in my room right now," I said, grabbing my suitcase before the mother had a chance to. "If anything's missing, I'll let you know. And we can make Edwy give them back."

"Nobody can make the Watanabonesets do anything," the father muttered.

"The Freds made them give up Edwy for twelve years, didn't they?" I retorted, without even thinking about it.

I believe if I'd been close enough to the mother, she would have slapped me again. But I'd already yanked my suitcase away, toward my room. I was already three steps away.

I left the mother and the father just standing there, stricken.

CHAPTER
NINETEEN

Once I was in the room Bobo and I shared, I unzipped my suitcase and slowly began lifting each item out. Somehow I knew the mother and the father would leave me alone. And it felt almost like a sacred ceremony for me, touching the things I'd last touched in Fredtown.

I didn't want it to end.

I piled books and school supplies in one corner, and clothing along the back wall. Here was the dress I'd worn the night of the school talent show; here were the heavy leggings I wore on the rare occasions when a cold wind swept down from the mountains into Fredtown. Here was the solar calculator I'd been so proud of receiving at the end of fifth grade— the Freds always said you had to prove you could work with numbers in your head before you could be trusted with owning a machine to do it for you. I'd always thought Edwy was better than me in math, but I'd earned my calculator first.

I reached the bottom of the suitcase too quickly. Even

after I emptied it, I kept it open. I knew I wasn't missing anything—everything I'd put into it back in Fredtown was already out and arranged along the walls of my new room. It didn't look like Edwy or his supposedly thieving family had stolen anything, and part of me wanted to go out and inform the father and mother of that. But I kept sitting there, kept running my hands along the suitcase's wrinkled lining, just in case there was some tiny item I'd forgotten about.

Something jabbed against my hand. It was something tucked under a loose edge of the lining. I tugged at the thing jabbing me—it was a piece of paper wrapped in on itself like a miniature cone.

From my Fred-parents? I thought.

My heart beat faster. Of course they wouldn't have sent me back home—to a home they even suspected might still be dangerous—without giving me a way out. A safety net of sorts. This was probably some secret way of reaching them, some secret number to call in case of emergency. Never mind that I hadn't seen a single phone since I'd left Fredtown. Never mind that there might be complications calling some-place so far away. I would be able to unwrap this paper and look at their message and get in touch with them right away. Because this was an emergency.

My real mother slapped me! I could tell my Fred-parents. *Something really bad happened here, and I think something bad might happen again! I'm worried about Bobo!*

And they would understand instantly. They would come and retrieve Bobo and me, and all the other kids, too. We could live the rest of our lives in Fredtown and we would always be safe.

With trembling hands, I began unrolling the tiny paper. Finally it lay flat in my hand. There were words written on the paper, words in handwriting I recognized instantly.

But the handwriting didn't belong to either of my Fred-parents.

It belonged to Edwy.

ONCE EVERYONE IN YOUR HOUSE IS ASLEEP TONIGHT, SNEAK OUT AND MEET ME. THERE'S SOMETHING I HAVE TO SHOW YOU.

CHAPTER
TWENTY

I don't do things like this, I told myself. *I'm not a sneaky person.*

It was night now, full dark. I was lying on the floor beside Bobo, and I could hear how his breathing had settled into the long, slow, contented pattern of sleep. I was pretty sure the mother and the father had fallen asleep too. Through the house's thin walls, I could hear two faltering versions of snoring—one more of a gasping snort, one deeper and gruff-sounding. Even in their sleep, the parents sounded angry.

And I was awake and trying to decide whether or not to sneak out and meet Edwy.

Back in Fredtown, I wouldn't have thought twice about Edwy's note. I would have crumpled it in my hand and thrown it away. I would have thought, *Oh, that Edwy! Trying to get me in trouble, just like him!*

Back in Fredtown, Edwy wouldn't have sent me a note

like that. He would have known I couldn't be tempted to follow it.

But here . . .

What if Edwy found out more about the bad thing that happened before and might happen again? What if sneaking out is the only way I can find out what I need to know to protect Bobo?

Why wasn't right and wrong as easy as it had always seemed back in Fredtown?

I sighed—too loudly. For a moment Bobo's breathing stuttered, and I was afraid I'd awakened him. Then he rolled toward me, hugged my shoulder in his sleep, and went back to breathing evenly.

Maybe Bobo holding on to me should have made me think, *I can't sneak out now! I have to stay with Bobo!*

But his arm flung so trustingly across my shoulder reminded me how much he depended on me, how much my Fred-parents were relying on me to take care of him and all the other children. It wasn't conceited to think that after the Freds had found out that none of them would be allowed to come home with us, I was their only hope. It was just . . . reality.

Silently I eased Bobo's arm off me and slid out from under the blanket. I didn't want Bobo waking up and realizing I was gone, so I grabbed a pile of my clothes from beside the wall and stuffed them under the blanket in a vaguely Rosi-shaped way. The deception wouldn't be very convincing if Bobo woke up and started talking to me—or if the mother came into the room and turned on a light. But it would trick anyone who glanced quickly and sleepily at the shape under the blanket. It would give Bobo something to cuddle against and feel comforted by until I came back.

Home is turning me into a sneaky person, I thought.

I tiptoed out of the room. After every step I paused and listened, because it wasn't too late to turn back. What if the father's enhanced hearing worked equally well whether he was asleep or awake?

The snores from the back of the house kept coming, gruff and angry.

I reached the front door and eased the latch open. I inched the door apart from the doorframe.

The hinges creaked and I froze, straining my ears to listen for snores.

Still there, still angry . . .

I stepped outside and pulled the door shut behind me.

Edwy was waiting in the shadows.

"I was about to give up," he whispered.

"I had to make sure everyone was asleep," I whispered back.

"You would," Edwy said.

At first I took that as an insult—Edwy acting disgusted that I was careful and meticulous, just as he was always disgusted back in Fredtown when I did my homework properly and made him look bad for scrawling down any old answer.

I almost turned around and went back into the house. But then he stepped out of the shadows and his eyes glinted for a moment in the dim moonlight. And there was something in his gaze that I'd never noticed before—admiration? trust?

Whatever it was made me step up beside Edwy. But I also put a finger to my lips.

"We shouldn't talk unless we have to," I whispered.

Edwy nodded. He handed me a pair of socks and pantomimed putting them over his shoes.

Oh, to muffle the sounds of our footsteps . . .

Edwy was good at being sneaky. He had a lot more practice at it than I did.

I slipped the socks over my own shoes. I thought about how Fred-mama would have fretted about holes growing in the socks, about wasting precious resources.

It's not a waste if this helps protect Bobo and the other kids, I thought with a firmness that surprised me. I felt like I was talking back to Fred-mama from a distance of thousands of kilometers.

Edwy and I crept forward, through the near-total darkness,

along the street full of tumbledown houses. We reached the creek and turned right, the opposite way from downtown.

"Nobody lives near the creek, so I think it's safe to talk now," Edwy whispered.

I could have said, *So what are you showing me?* I could have said, *Why couldn't this have waited until tomorrow?* I could have said, *Have you ever heard of a parent slapping a child? Have you ever heard of anyone treating someone differently just because of the color of her eyes?* But Fred customs required a clearing of the air after any insult or slight, and somehow I couldn't let go of every bit of Fredtown behavior.

"I'm sorry the . . . my . . . the adults never thanked you for bringing the suitcases," I said. "I'm sorry they acted so mean about your family."

Edwy shrugged, a motion I could barely see in the darkness.

"That's okay," he said. "They were right. My family did steal your suitcases. I just stole them back."

I gasped. But Edwy grinned, his teeth gleaming white in the moonlight.

"Edwy, that's not funny!" I said. "You need to tell someone! I know you wouldn't want to tattle, but you shouldn't have to live in an environment like that! You have a right to—to—"

"Rosi, Rosi, Rosi," Edwy said, still grinning. I didn't

know if he meant to sound like my Fred-parents or not, but it made my heart ache a little. "We're not in Fredtown anymore. Who would I tell? I mean, who else? I just told you."

My heart seemed to skip a beat. Edwy meant that he'd chosen me as his confidant, as the person he trusted to help him right a wrong. He was treating me like a grown-up, like a Fred.

I felt the burden of responsibility. How could either of us fix a problem like this?

How could we fix anything about our hometown when we didn't understand what had happened here?

"Every child has the right to grow up in safety and security, without fear and without lies," I said numbly, quoting another principle of Fredtown.

"Yeah, well, if nobody lies to us and nobody tells us the truth either, *that* just leaves us—what was that word the man on the plane used? It leaves us stupid," Edwy said. "It makes us dumb, stupid idiots."

I cringed, hearing him say those words.

"Ignorant," I corrected him. "Just because we don't know things, that doesn't mean our brains don't work. It doesn't mean we can't *learn* what we need to know."

Edwy just looked at me.

"Either way, do *you* think we're safe and secure here?" he asked.

Fredtown customs required being optimistic and looking on the bright side and making the best of things. But somehow, sneaking around in the dark seemed to give me permission to tell Edwy the truth. It wasn't just the darkness that scared me.

"No," I whispered.

"That's what I think too," Edwy whispered back.

What could I say to that? For a while we walked along the creek without speaking. The path seemed oddly overgrown. The moon kept disappearing behind the roiling clouds in the sky, and for long moments we could only feel our way tentatively, grasping for tree trunks and branches.

"I gave up on the fishing this afternoon," Edwy finally whispered. "Why bother doing something you know you're going to fail at?"

"Because you can never know for sure," I argued. "Because—"

"Rosi, *listen*," Edwy said, and something in his voice silenced me. In the darkness, when I wasn't looking directly at him, he sounded almost as young as Bobo. I could relate to him the way I had when he was younger and we were best friends.

"I'm listening," I said.

Edwy nodded impatiently.

"Anyhow, this afternoon, I knew it was too soon to go

home, because then everyone would know I'd given up," he said. "So I started looking around. I wanted to see everything in this town with my own eyes."

I could respect that. I didn't remind him it fit with the Fredtown principle about paying attention so you'd learn something every day.

"I saw the places where all the houses are nice and you could just tell that everybody had a lot of money," he said. "Even if they stole it."

Maybe he was trying to make me laugh. But I didn't.

"I saw places where the houses were poor and falling down, and the people walking around didn't even seem to own shoes," he said.

Like where Bobo and I live, I thought. I hadn't realized I should be grateful that at least we had shoes.

"And then I saw . . . this," Edwy said.

He took my shoulder and aimed me away from the creek and the sheltering line of trees.

All I could see was darkness. I put my hands out in front of my face and felt only empty air.

"Edwy, there's nothing here," I said.

"We're walking on ash now," he said. "Feel it."

He took my arm and—with more gentleness than I would have thought him capable of—pulled me down into a crouch so I could touch my fingers to the ground.

It did feel like ash beneath my fingertips. Old, cold, dead ash.

"Wait for the moon to come back out," Edwy whispered. "You'll see. The ash, the burned place—it goes on and on. . . ."

I shivered just at the tone of his voice. The glow of the moon was muted, right at the edge of a cloud. Very slowly, the cloud began to slip away, releasing more light. I saw hillocks and shadowy bumps ahead of us.

"There was a house that burned back in Fredtown, remember?" I told Edwy. "Someone forgot to blow out a candle. But the family was safe because they had smoke detectors. And we started having Fire Safety Day at school every year after that."

I wondered if my house here had smoke detectors. Probably not. I would have to talk to the mother and the father about that.

"*One* house in Fredtown burned," Edwy said. "And the family rebuilt it right away. My Fred-dad was the architect, so I heard all about the plans. That was a long time ago. I bet you can't even remember which house it was now."

He was right. I couldn't.

"I don't think you'll be able to see until the moon's all the way out, but probably a hundred houses burned here," Edwy said. "And it was a long time ago here, too, because some of the ruined houses have trees growing out of the middle of them. And it doesn't look like anybody has tried to rebuild."

I stood up. The moon was still half hidden, but there was enough light now that the hillocks and bumps ahead of me were transformed into fallen beams and collapsed, half-burned walls. We were in a wasteland, a cemetery of old, dead, decaying houses.

"What happened to all the people who lived here?" I asked. "Did they leave after their houses burned, and they never came back?"

"Or," Edwy whispered, "did they all die?"

"Yeah, and it was those Freds who stopped us," the first man answered. "We don't have to worry about *them* anymore."

My heart gave a little leap of dismay. I didn't know what these men were talking about. They spoke as carelessly and cruelly as the men who'd brought us from Fredtown, but I'd seen those men leaving with the plane. Like they were supposed to. These men seemed to be from my hometown; they'd said, "We've got the children back."

And, listening in the darkness, I could hear that there was a difference in the way these men pronounced their words. A different accent. The men on the plane had made their words into weapons, sharp and cutting and so different from the gentle way Freds talked. But the mother, the father, these men—really, everyone I'd encountered in my hometown—they all spoke as if they had burrs or thistles in their mouths. Something painful they had to talk around.

What happened the "last time," when these men were "so close to succeeding"? Was it something dating back twelve years?

I couldn't be sure. But if the Freds had stopped them before, I was almost certain I would want the Freds to stop them now.

"The trick is to achieve victory in one fell swoop," the other man said. "Before the enemy knows what's happening."

"And that's why we're meeting out here," a third voice said, in a way that seemed to settle the argument. "So the enemy has no warning."

For a moment I could hear nothing but the thud of footsteps. Were the three men going to find us? Should we start crawling away?

The footsteps veered off to the right. I heard the creak of a door opening and closing. I started to sit up, but Edwy pulled me back down.

"Shh," he hissed. "There's more coming. Can't you hear them?"

Now I did. Was this a larger group? Or just louder? It was hard to separate out the sound of individual footsteps, but I guessed there might have been five or six people headed our way now.

"Have you seen how those kids look at you?" A voice floated toward us. "Especially *certain* ones. The enemy's children. It's like they're not afraid of anyone or anything."

"They've got no respect," someone else said, like he was agreeing.

"We'll show them," a voice replied. "They'll learn to fear us."

Someone else laughed, in a way that shot chills through me.

"We can't let them hurt anybody," I whispered to Edwy.

Edwy replied by putting his hand over my mouth. When

CHAPTER
TWENTY-TWO

We raced toward the creek path, scrambling over logs and burned beams, tripping and immediately pulling each other back up.

Was someone chasing us already—closing in on us—or were we just hearing the echoes of our own footsteps? Everything seemed too loud: our feet slapping against the ground, twigs snapping underfoot, my own breathing rasping in and out, my own pulse thudding in my ears.

"Put your hands up over your face so you won't get scratches!" Edwy hissed at me. "So they can't identify us that way!"

He thought we could escape. He thought we should worry about getting scrapes and scratches on our faces, which would be noticeable tomorrow.

I'd always thought Edwy was so gloomy and pessimistic, but I felt grateful to him for being able to think so hopefully, even as we ran. Even though *I* was certain we were about to be caught, I put my hands up, and a second later began to feel branches and leaves and twigs slashing them.

"Good call," I tried to mutter to Edwy, but was rewarded with a mouthful of leaves.

I angled my hands differently, spread my fingers wider, and kept running.

The moon went behind a cloud again, and I was torn between gratitude that now we were harder to see and fear because now I couldn't see either. The loss of moonlight did make me notice dimmer lights up ahead, off to the side of the creek.

"That's the start of the houses that people still live in," Edwy whispered in my ear. "Your street is the third one in. We'll split apart there—you sneak home as quietly as you can, and I'll make some noise so we're sure they keep following me instead."

"Edwy, *no*," I objected, trying not to pant. "I don't want you in danger either."

Edwy didn't say anything for a few seconds. I hoped he was coming up with a safer plan. We reached the third street in, and suddenly he turned and yelled into the darkness behind us: "You can't catch me!"

"Edwy!" I protested.

"Too late to complain about my plan now," he said. He

shoved me toward my street. "Now go! Fast! Don't waste the chance I just gave you!"

I was so mad at Edwy.

Fredtown customs would have required me to stand there and talk out my anger until it was gone—and until I'd convinced him to work with me on a totally different plan, one that was safe for both of us. But he was already several steps ahead of me, crashing noisily into the creek. Crashing noisily *on purpose*.

"Think of . . . your brother!" he called back to me. "What would happen to him if you got caught? Go!"

That Edwy—he was going to keep yelling and attracting attention as long as I stood there. I turned and ran away from the creek, toward my street. And then, because running was too loud, as soon as I reached the first house I slipped silently into the shadows it cast off to the side. I tiptoed behind it, and then around the back of the next house. And the next. And the next.

I could hear noise from back at the creek, but it wasn't very loud.

The men who'd been chasing us—and were still chasing Edwy—evidently didn't want to be heard either. I could make out the swish of branches being pushed aside and swiped away, but maybe to the people in the nearest houses it only sounded like a peaceful breeze moving leaves around.

Maybe Edwy splashing out into the creek had sounded like possums or fish or even snakes—who would want to investigate that? The only really loud noise had been Edwy shouting, "You can't catch me!" And even that might be dismissed as children playing. The father and the mother hadn't wanted me to go out after dark, but maybe other parents didn't care. Maybe it'd been so long since most of the town had been around children, they wouldn't be surprised at all to hear kids out playing in the middle of the night. . . .

All the way home, tiptoeing and creeping and darting from shadow to shadow, I kept telling myself that Edwy was smart and careful enough to make it home safely too. Maybe he was making noise on one side of the creek and then silently darting back to the other. Maybe he was already turning down his own street. Maybe he was going faster than me. Maybe he was already home, safe in his own bed.

It was kind of easier to worry about Edwy than to worry about myself.

My street was creepier than ever in the darkness, now that I was alone. Its jumbled, broken-down houses cast eerie shadows. Once or twice I stopped moving entirely and told myself I was only being cautious, plotting my next step. Really, I was paralyzed with fear.

The mother and the father seemed so afraid of letting me go to the airport to pick up the suitcases after dark. . . . They were so terrified of Edwy's knock at the door before they knew it was Edwy. . . . What if the men chasing us just now understood that Edwy was trying to trick them? What if they knew to turn down this street and follow me?

I forced myself to start tiptoeing again with the same words that Edwy had shouted to me back at the creek: *Think of your brother! What would happen to him if you got caught?*

Finally, I just focused on my brother's name with every step:

Bobo.

Bobo.

Bobo.

I reached my own house. I didn't care that it looked like it might fall down at any minute. I didn't care that it needed paint. All I wanted was to get back through that door. I pushed it open, grateful that I'd left it unlatched.

The hinges squeaked again. In the darkness, they sounded as loud as the yowling of a cat, as loud as Edwy screaming, "You can't catch me!"

Only this was like the hinges screaming, *You can catch me! Catch me now!*

I waited, listening for the parents' snore. There was one of them—fluttery and faltering and furious, even in sleep. The mother's. I listened for the father's deeper, gruffer snore too.

It wasn't there.

I heard a creak at the back of the house. I heard heavy footsteps.

Just be quiet, I told myself. *Maybe he didn't hear the door. Maybe he's just getting up to go to the privy.*

The footsteps were coming toward me.

Don't worry. It's not like he's going to see me. Just—get out of the way.

I inched off to the side, trying to feel my way back to my own room.

"Girl!" the father hissed. "I can hear that that's you! What are you doing? Why did you just open the front door?"

CHAPTER
TWENTY-THREE

I had to think fast.

I had to think like Edwy.

"I—I thought I heard something outside," I said. "I just wanted to see—"

The father was by my side in a flash. For a second I wondered how he had navigated past the kitchen table and chairs so quickly in the dark. Then I remembered that the house was always dark for him.

"What did you hear?" he asked, his voice a stressed-out rumble.

"Maybe someone running?" I said, trying to sound doubtful in an ordinary way, not an "I'm totally lying to you" way.

But maybe there would be someone running near our house, right outside. Maybe I did have to worry about that.

The father jerked me out of the way and pressed his ear against the door.

"Shh. Let me listen. . . ." He kept his ear there for a long time before he finally pulled away. "Are you *sure* you heard someone running outside?"

"No," I said. "Maybe I just dreamed it, and then when I woke up I got all confused and thought the sound was real. . . ."

Either of my Fred-parents would have patted my shoulder and nodded sagely at that explanation and said something like *Oh, yes, sometimes it is difficult to distinguish between dreams and reality when you first wake up. It's good you realize now that that was only a dream. See? Nothing to worry about.*

But the father clutched my arm and kept . . . well, I would have said that he kept staring at me, but it was more like even without being able to see me, he was making sure I kept my gaze fastened on him.

It was like he could tell somehow that I was still straining to listen to whatever was going on outside. I was still listening for running feet, for the men who'd been chasing Edwy and me.

"If that ever happens again—if you ever hear anything suspicious outside," he began, speaking in a low, urgent voice, as if we were in the middle of a crisis, "whatever you do, do *not* open the front door. Don't even look out the front window. And if you hear people outside running or . . . screaming or . . . sounding afraid, get your mother and Bobo and me—or whoever's here in the house. Don't look for us outside. Let's hope we're all here when it happens. Because then you come over here, as quick as you can, . . ."

He walked me over to the chair he usually sat in. In the darkness, I bumped against it.

"And you bend down, and you pull away the rug, and *this* is where we hide," he said. "All together."

He pulled me down toward the floor in front of the chair and shoved the rug away, just as he'd described. And then he was holding my hand against a board, which he lifted and slid to the side. I couldn't see, of course, but he made me reach down into the cold, dark gaping hole beneath the floor.

It felt like a tomb.

"You pull the board back over the top of you," he said. "There's a little nail you loop the rug over so it will lie flat when everything's back in place. . . . Can you feel it?"

He took my hand and rubbed my fingers against the board. I did feel the nail.

"Okay," I gasped. "Okay. But why . . . what . . . ? When do you think we'd ever need this?"

"We didn't have it the last time," he said. He was still right beside me; his hand still hovered over mine. But somehow he sounded far, far away. "If only we had . . ."

I waited. He didn't go on.

"What happened?" I whispered. "The 'last time'? What are you talking about?"

I thought of his one empty shirtsleeve, his sightless eyes, the way the mother's face seemed frozen in pain. I thought about the men meeting out in the shack in the wasteland, the way they said they would have succeeded "the last time" if it hadn't been for the Freds.

I thought about how there weren't any kids older than me and Edwy, and how the Freds had kept us and all the younger kids away from here for the past twelve years.

Were all those things connected?

Were they the reason the father thought we needed a hidden tomb beneath our house?

The father ran his one hand over his face. Maybe he was wiping away tears. It was too hard to tell in the dark.

"Never mind," the father said. "You don't need to hear about the last time. Just—be ready. Remember."

He shoved the board back in place, straightened the rug over top of it.

"Go back to bed," he ordered. "Before you wake up everyone."

"All right," I said.

I crept past him and back into the room I shared with Bobo. I slid under the blanket and shoved my piled-up clothes—my decoy Rosi—out of the way.

And then I lay there, thinking about the wasteland of burned-down houses Edwy had shown me, about the likelihood that Edwy could have given himself away trying to cover my escape, about the fact that the father thought something so awful was going to happen to us as a family that the best thing we could do was bury ourselves under the floor like so many corpses.

What if we hid down there and there was a fire? I wondered. *What if the father doesn't even know about all of the burned-down houses, so he hasn't thought of that danger?*

I told myself to think about happy things instead.

I had escaped. The men chasing us hadn't caught me, and the father never guessed that I'd been outside.

And Edwy had been kind to me.

Dangerously kind.

CHAPTER
TWENTY-FOUR

I was so slow and sluggish in the morning.

I think the father could tell that as soon as I stumbled out of my room. He was sitting at the kitchen table, and he immediately turned his head in my direction and scowled. He took a long drink from a mug, then thumped it down on the table.

"The girl should stay here today and help you clean house," he growled to the mother, who was standing at the stove, frying something in a pan. "I don't need her downtown."

I felt as though he had slapped me now too.

But then he inclined his head ever so slightly toward the rug on the floor in front of his usual chair, and I wondered if I'd misunderstood.

Was he trying to tell me that the bad things he feared might happen today? Was he saying he wanted me to stay home so I could hide under the floor with Bobo and the mother if we had to?

What would happen to him off in the marketplace, by himself?

"Oh, uh . . . ," I began.

Bobo, who'd been standing on a chair by the stove, came running over and wrapped his arms around my legs.

"Rosi can play with me all day!" he exclaimed happily.

"I think we'll need to work some too," I said weakly. My brain kept jumping around, lighting on topics I couldn't bring up in front of Bobo. Like the hole under the floor. And Edwy. How could I make sure Edwy had gotten home safely last night if I was stuck in the house with the mother and Bobo all day?

I realized what I could say.

"Wait—isn't it Monday?" I asked. "Don't we have school?"

The mother stayed bent over the frying pan, but her back stiffened. The father clenched his teeth.

"There's no school this week," the mother said, finally turning around. "It's still . . . holiday."

"Hurray!" Bobo said, jumping up and down. "I hope holiday lasts forever!"

"But school is . . . ," I began. I could have gone on with one of the Freds' principles about the importance of education. But those probably would have made the mother and the father angry all over again. And I couldn't say what I was really thinking: *School is the best way to check on the other kids, to make sure they're all okay. Especially Edwy.*

"School is *not* my favorite thing!" Bobo finished for me. "Except for recess. And lunch. And the games . . ."

I forced out a laugh that sounded too high and fake, even to my own ears.

"Bobo, you love everything about school except when you have to sit still," I told him.

"Yeah, but that's *awful!*" Bobo said. "The worst thing ever!"

The mother stood frozen by the stove, the frying pan still clutched in her hand. The father's jawline was clenched like rock. I didn't know why mentioning school had set them off. But it was like they were in a totally different world from Bobo, who was still bouncing up and down in his own little happy bubble, where he could play all day and the worst thing he could possibly imagine was having to sit still for five minutes.

I was caught between the two, the parents' world and Bobo's. I had to keep Bobo protected and safe and innocent and in his little happy bubble. I was the only one who could do that.

The mother slid fried eggs onto a plate.

"Come on, Bobo," she called. "Your breakfast is ready."

"Oh, goody!" he cried, letting go of me and racing back toward the table.

The father let out a sigh and scraped back his chair. He left an empty plate behind.

"And I'm off to work," he said heavily.

He picked up the bag of apples he'd carried home the day before and headed for the door. As he brushed past me, I wanted to say, *Don't worry. I'll make sure Bobo and the mother get into the hole if anything bad happens.* I wanted to say, *If anything bad happens at the marketplace, make sure you stay safe too.*

But I didn't say anything. I just watched him go.

After he pulled the door shut behind him, the mother said sharply to me, "Make yourself some breakfast, Rosi. There's eggs you can have, too. Surely you know how to fix them yourself."

I did know how to fry eggs using the stove at my Fredparents' house back in Fredtown. But I had seen actual flames under the mother's cast-iron pan, and I wasn't used to that. Flames made me think of the ash and burned houses from the night before, which made me think of Edwy, which made me worry all over again.

"That's okay," I told the mother. "I think I'll just eat the sandwich you made for me yesterday."

She pursed her lips in a sour way, as if I'd been trying to annoy her by refusing to cook my own eggs. Or by having failed to eat the sandwich yesterday.

I unwrapped it from the cloth that was still sitting on the counter. I sat down beside Bobo and took a bite. The bread was dry and hard, and the layer of butter in the middle seemed slimy and rancid. I had to force myself to chew and swallow.

Who cares about food when all of us may be in danger? I thought. *When I don't even know what I need to protect Bobo from? When Edwy might have been caught last night? When we know those men who chased us were plotting something....*

I put the sandwich down on the table.

"Who's in charge here?" I asked.

"In this *house?*" the mother asked, her voice sharp. "Your father, when he's here. Me, when he's not."

I refrained from telling her how much Fred-mama and Fred-daddy had always said they were equal partners. I didn't think it would help right now.

"No, I mean, in this town," I said. "Is there a mayor? A town council? A city manager? A police force?"

Those were all things we'd talked about in school back in Fredtown.

The mother let out a disgusted snort.

"As if any of those things would help," she muttered. "I'll tell you who *isn't* in charge in this town. *Us.* We have to just put up with how things are run. Try to survive somehow. That's all any of us can do."

I wondered if the father had told her about showing me the hole under the floor. I thought maybe he had.

The mother cast a glance at Bobo, who was obliviously gobbling down his eggs.

"That's a good appetite," she said admiringly. Then she turned back to me. "If you aren't going to eat, you may as well start work. You can do the dishes."

I rose and went to the sink. Maybe if I got the work done early, I could find an excuse to go out and look for Edwy.

But as the day wore on, I despaired of there being any end to the work the mother assigned me. I washed and dried and put away the dishes. I fed the chickens in the backyard. I weeded the garden. I scrubbed the floor. I washed sheets and towels and shirts and hung them on a line to dry.

While I worked at the clothesline, the mother stood at the fence, talking in a low voice with someone I couldn't even see in the neighbor's yard. When the mother turned to walk back toward me, I thought maybe she'd say, "Rosi, let me introduce you to our next-door neighbor." I thought maybe we'd all sit down together for tea and cakes. That was how things would have gone in Fredtown. But the mother scowled at me worse than ever. She snatched one of the father's shirts I'd just stretched smooth and pinned in place.

"Oh, no! It's missing a button!" she cried, crumpling

the shirt's collar. Her hands shook, as if that missing button made her furious. Or—as if I did.

"I'm sorry," I said. "I didn't notice. Where—?"

She yanked the shirt from the line, popping the clothespins off. It was almost like she didn't want me to see.

"Never mind," she snapped. "I'll go down to the market to buy a new one."

I saw my chance.

"I can go," I volunteered.

"No!" she cried, as if my offer made her even angrier. "You stay here with Bobo. And . . . wash the windows when you're done there."

She rushed toward the house, and I followed her in. I probably should have known it was hopeless, but this could be the only opportunity I'd get today to find out about Edwy.

"Are you sure?" I said, trying to sound guileless. "The market's a long way to walk, and it's gotten really hot out. But I don't mind going for you."

The mother made her lips all thin and disapproving, the same expression she'd been giving me all day.

"Are you trying to shirk?" she asked. "You know I'm in charge here when your father's away. *I'll* decide who stays and who goes!"

"I was just trying to help," I muttered.

The mother acted like she didn't hear me.

She put on a hat and got her purse and stepped out the front door.

I didn't hurry back out to the clothesline or off to wash the windows. I just stood there, gazing back and forth between the space under the kitchen table where Bobo was pretending to sail his toy boat and the spot on the floor where I knew the secret hiding place lay. It wouldn't be safe to go off and leave Bobo here by himself. Would it be safe to go out to look for Edwy and take Bobo with me?

I'd never had to make a decision like this back in Fredtown.

I have to keep Bobo safe . . .

I didn't even know where the danger lay. And knowledge was power.

"Hey, Bobo, how would you like to go out for a walk?" I asked.

"I'm playing with my boat," Bobo said. "Boats can't walk."

Seriously? Now I was going to have to argue with Bobo to get him to budge?

I figured out how to do it.

"I bet Edwy would love to play with the boat with you," I said. "I just meant a walk to Edwy's house."

"You'll let me play with Edwy?" Bobo cried, scrambling out from under the table. "Hurray!"

Bobo was by my side in an instant, his toy boat bumping along behind him.

I hoped Bobo didn't notice that my hands shook as I unlatched the door. I hoped he didn't notice that I peered around cautiously before stepping outside.

I looked down, and Bobo was squinting suspiciously up at me.

"How come you're letting me play with Edwy?" he asked. "I thought you didn't like Edwy."

"I didn't like how Edwy acted sometimes back in Fredtown," I replied, trying to keep my voice even. "It was never that I disliked Edwy."

This was exactly something that my Fred-parents might have said.

"So now that we're home, Edwy is good?" Bobo asked.

How was I supposed to answer that? *No, but now that I've met worse people, Edwy doesn't seem so bad?* Or *No, I'm just desperate?*

"Edwy does seem to be behaving better here," I said. Was that true?

I realized I didn't care the same way I used to. I just hoped Edwy was safe.

Bobo bounced along behind me as we walked down the street. It was dusty and empty and silent, and I wondered if other people knew something we didn't. Did our neighbors have hiding spaces in their houses like the one the father had revealed to me last night? Were they all cowering under their floors, and should Bobo and I be huddled under our floor right now too?

I thought about how it would terrify Bobo to be hustled into the darkness under the floorboard. I thought about how difficult it would be to explain the need to hide and be quiet, if it came to that.

Stop scaring yourself, I thought. *Your neighbors are all just . . . out working or shopping at the market. That's why the street is empty and quiet.*

But I didn't know our neighbors. I didn't really know anything about where they were or what they were doing.

Do they have brown eyes or green eyes? I wondered, and then immediately forced that thought from my mind.

We reached the place where the street dead-ended by the creek, and I told Bobo, "We'll walk along the creek until we get to the spot where I saw Edwy yesterday."

Then, I thought, we could turn off down the nearest street and hope that that was where Edwy lived. Wouldn't Edwy have fished in the portion of the creek nearest to his house? Wouldn't he be that lazy?

"Water!" Bobo cried delightedly. "Which will sail downstream faster? A leaf or a twig or my boat?"

The water was so shallow and slow-moving, I thought it would probably be safe to let him try out that little science experiment. Then I realized the problem with that.

"The water's flowing the wrong way," I told Bobo. "We need to turn *that* way, toward Edwy's house"—I pointed to the left—"and the water would carry your boat in the other direction."

"Oh," Bobo said, slumping dejectedly against my side. "Maybe when we find Edwy, *he'll* come and play with me in the water."

"Maybe," I said. "Or we could just try that experiment on the way home."

"Oh, yes!" Bobo exclaimed, skipping ahead of me now.

Eventually the creek widened, and I thought that was the spot where I'd seen Edwy the day before. I lured Bobo away from the creek with the promise "It's not much farther now."

We ended up on a street full of mansions, like something out of a fairy tale.

Back in Fredtown, the houses had all been about the same size. Oh, a family with five kids might have had an extra bedroom or two. And Cana's Fred-daddy was a chef, so her Fred-family had had the biggest kitchen in town. But the differences were so slight I bet a lot of the younger kids hadn't even noticed.

The houses on this street were twenty or thirty times bigger than the house Bobo and I lived in here. I saw *windows* that were bigger than some of the houses on our street.

And these houses were all surrounded by fences.

"Does Edwy climb a fence every time he wants to go in or out of his yard?" Bobo murmured.

I couldn't tell if Bobo thought that would be fun or annoying.

"I guess there are gates," I muttered back. I noticed what seemed to be hinges in the nearest fence, and I gently pushed against one of the wrought-iron bars.

It didn't budge. The gate was locked.

I'd pictured casually asking someone where Edwy lived, and then casually walking up to his front door. What if Bobo and I had to climb a fence to get *to* him?

What if Edwy had needed to climb a fence to get back to his house last night, and that little complication had meant that the scary men had captured him?

I pushed that thought out of my mind. If Bobo and I needed to climb a fence to find Edwy, we would. I looked at the nearest fence, with its spiked peaks towering a good four or five feet over my head, and I changed my mind: *Well, I can climb a fence. But Bobo could fall. I'll just have to talk him into waiting for a few minutes out in the street. . . .*

"Look—a W!" Bobo exclaimed. "Isn't that what Edwy's last name starts with?"

Bobo pointed to a fancy set of curlicues embedded in the wrought iron of a fence on the opposite side of the street. He was right—it was a shining golden W glowing out from the black fence. The W, I realized, was on a gate.

And this gate was the only one I could see that hung open.

"Good job for spotting that, Bobo!" I praised him. "You're right about Edwy's last name! Let's go see if that's where Edwy lives!"

We crossed the street and walked through the gate. It led to a vast circular driveway where four sleek black cars were parked in a row.

"Ooh," Bobo breathed, staring at the cars. "Why don't the mother and the father have cars like that? Why didn't our Fred-mama and Fred-daddy?"

"I don't know," I muttered. I thought about how Edwy had said there were streets in our hometown where people didn't even own shoes. I thought about how the parents thought Edwy's parents were thieves. I thought about how Edwy had *said* his parents were thieves.

Is that how they'd gotten these cars?

Bobo began bouncing up and down, like he always did when he was excited.

"Will Edwy take us for a ride in one of his cars?" Bobo asked.

"Bobo, you know it's rude to ask for something like that," I said. My voice came out sounding even sterner than I meant it to. "You can only go for a ride if Edwy offers."

"Oh," Bobo said, deflating a little and bouncing less. "Right."

We had to climb five steep steps to get to the front door. I had to pull Bobo up by the elbows.

There was a shiny brass knocker in the middle of the door. I lifted it and let it fall again, letting it make a heavy thud against the wood.

The door opened, revealing a woman in a black dress and lacy apron.

"Excuse me," I said. "Are you Mrs. Watanaboneset? Edwy's mother?"

The woman frowned and glanced quickly over her shoulder before looking back at me. Was she afraid of someone or something behind her, out of my sight past the large marble entryway?

"I'm the *maid*," the woman said.

I thought of the young maids and maidens of fairy tales. Sometimes, in stories, girls had to be rescued by knights or princes, or they got their turn rescuing knights or princes who were in danger themselves. Was that what this woman meant?

The woman tilted her head, as if she could see I didn't understand.

"I work here," the woman said. "I dust and clean and answer the door. I'm *not* Mrs. Watanaboneset."

"Oh," I said. "But is this where Edwy Watanaboneset lives? Can he, uh, come out and play?"

The maid cast another fearful glance over her shoulder.

"Ed-wy!" Bobo started to call out into the cavern of all that marble ahead of us.

The maid clamped her hand over Bobo's mouth, muffling his cry.

"Shh," she hissed at us. "Go away and don't come back. Don't tell anyone you're friends with Edwy. Maybe then you'll be safe."

"What?" I said. "Is *Edwy* safe? Where is he?"

The maid pushed us away from the door. It took me a minute to realize she was backing us into a huge bush that stood beside the porch.

She was hiding us.

"Just go!" she insisted.

I glanced down at Bobo and felt torn once again. The maid's strange behavior was frightening, and I didn't want Bobo to be scared. Already his eyes were wide and confused. I couldn't let him shift into terror.

But Edwy and I had promised to look out for each other, and I had to keep my promise.

After all, he had protected me the night before.

"We won't go until we know what happened to Edwy," I said, stubbornly bracing my feet in a way that kept the maid from shoving me off the porch. I clutched Bobo to my side and squared my shoulders.

The maid was no taller than me. She didn't look strong enough to overpower us both.

"I'm only trying to help you," the maid whispered. Bobo and I were still on the porch, yes, but the maid had my back pinned against the hard branches of the bush. "Didn't those Freds teach you to be afraid of anything? Didn't they teach you that sometimes fear is the only thing that will keep you alive?"

"The only thing we have to fear is fear itself," Bobo piped up. I was proud of him for remembering that principle of Fredtown.

The maid's eyes darted about like she thought he was crazy.

"Fine," she said. "I'll tell you, if that gets you to leave. Edwy was kidnapped. Nobody knows where he is."

CHAPTER TWENTY-FIVE

I gasped, and Bobo said, "Kidnapped? That only happens in stories. Stories people make up just to scare themselves for fun. Can't you stop being so silly?"

This woman—this maid—wasn't being silly. She was scared: scared for us and scared for Edwy and scared most of all for herself. That was why she kept looking back over her shoulder.

She did this one more time, casting a long gaze back through the open door.

"When did this happen?" I asked. "Was it last night? Because if it was, I should tell the police—" I remembered that I hadn't seen any evidence that there were police in this town. "Or whoever's in charge—"

"Don't tell anyone anything!" the woman said, her voice high and panicked. "And whatever you do, don't say you talked to me!"

She gave me a shove I wasn't expecting, and Bobo and I

both toppled off the side of the porch. The bush mostly held us up—we weren't in danger of anything worse than a few scrapes and scratches. But none of this made sense.

The maid stalked back into the house and slammed the door. Because the nearest window was open, I could hear her telling someone, "It was nobody. Just a couple of beggars."

A principle of Fredtown was that everybody was somebody. There was no such thing as an unimportant person.

Did beggars actually exist outside of stories?

"I didn't like her," Bobo said, sticking his lower lip out. He slid down the side of the bush, his feet landing in perfectly trimmed grass. "She was mean. Why does Edwy live with mean people?"

Was she mean? I wondered. *Or . . . did she honestly think she was helping us?*

"Edwy didn't choose who he lives with," I said. "Any more than we did."

"Everyone has choices," Bobo said, like he was correcting me, quoting another principle.

I gingerly lowered myself to the grass beside Bobo and brushed twigs and leaves off his clothes and mine. I looked up at the door again, shut tight. The big brass knocker seemed to taunt me, gleaming so brightly in the afternoon sunlight.

That isn't a choice, I told myself. *Even if I knock again, that woman won't let us in. I have to do something else to help Edwy.*

"Come on," I said, taking Bobo's hand.

"But—Edwy!" Bobo protested. "You said I could play with Edwy!"

"Think of this as . . . we're playing hide-and-seek with Edwy," I told him. "Or having a scavenger hunt, and Edwy is the prize."

"Ooh, I love scavenger hunts!" Bobo said. "What's the first clue?"

Why hadn't I just stuck with "hide-and-seek"?

"We have to look for it," I said.

Obligingly, Bobo began shoving aside branches of the bush we'd just climbed out of. I looked back at the enormous, forbidding house.

"It'd be too obvious for there to be clues at Edwy's house," I said. "We have to look somewhere else."

"Where?" Bobo asked.

In the place where there are likeliest to be answers, I thought. *Which means . . . the place where the most people are clustered together. The place the father didn't want me to go today.*

I swallowed a lump in my throat.

"Come on, Bobo," I said. "Let's go look for clues at the marketplace."

CHAPTER
TWENTY-SIX

We went back to walk along the creek, because that was the only way I knew to get to the marketplace. Bobo whined a little about going in the wrong direction again for sailing his boat, but then I got him to look for scavenger-hunt clues along the creek.

"Look, this branch is broken off like someone ran into it really, really fast," he said, pointing first at a bush, then to the ground. "And this grass is all smashed down, like a lot of people were running here."

I thought he was just goofing around, making up stories. But the grass was oddly mashed, and a lot of the branches sagged, half broken. Had there been a lot of running here the night before? Had the men chased Edwy past the turnoff for his own street?

What if he hadn't actually been kidnapped? What if he had just hidden from the men and was too scared to come out yet?

That didn't sound like Edwy. He wasn't afraid of anything.

"This is a hard scavenger hunt," Bobo complained, dragging his feet in the dirt. "Aren't there supposed to be *word* clues? Things written down that we can figure out?"

"I guess whoever set up this scavenger hunt thought you could handle a harder one now," I told him. "One without words."

"I'm not that grown-up," Bobo said, so serious it was almost comical. "I'm only little. I'm not ready for hard stuff."

Me neither, I thought. In my head I saw the mother's hand slapping my face, the ruins of all the burned houses, the hiding place under the floor. I didn't want to be ready for any of those things. How could anybody be ready for those things?

But I told Bobo, "That's why we're working on this together. That's why you have me to help you."

I wished I had someone to help me.

Maybe the father . . . ? I thought. *Or if the mother's still there . . .*

Would they help? Could I count on them to be that much like my Fred-parents?

I was still trying to formulate a plan when we reached the place where the creek curved like a hairpin and we needed to turn off toward the marketplace. I remembered how Meki, our old neighbor, had wanted to come out and give me a hug the day before, and how her father had yelled at me. I didn't want anyone yelling at Bobo.

"Piggyback ride the rest of the way!" I announced to Bobo. "And I'll gallop!"

"Hurray!" Bobo cried, clambering up onto my back.

He left muddy footprints on my skirt, but I didn't bother brushing them away. I took off, bouncing up and down, dodging the broken pieces of sidewalk.

By the time we got to the marketplace, my back ached and I was out of breath. And my knees were sore from all the times I'd stumbled and half fallen on the uneven pavement. But at least we hadn't run into anyone who yelled at us.

"That's a lot of people," Bobo whispered in my ear as he stared wide-eyed at the crowded market.

"No more than at the marketplace back in Fredtown," I told him, trying to sound soothing. If I'd counted, the numbers might have been the same as in Fredtown. But back in Fredtown the marketplace was always such a bright, cheery, welcoming place. People waited patiently in line; people took turns. People said, "Oh, no, no, you go first. I insist." Here, there was grabbing and shoving, elbowing and glaring. A bad feeling hung over the marketplace like a cloud.

You just think that because you're worried about Edwy, I told myself. *The people here just . . . practice different customs than in Fredtown. That's all.*

Still, I told Bobo, "You can keep riding on my back while we look around here. You don't have to be down where you can't see."

"Okay," Bobo said, tightening his grip around my neck. He nuzzled against my back. "And, Rosi? You don't have to keep pretending that we're doing a scavenger hunt. You can just look for Edwy."

It took my breath away that he'd figured me out.

Had he also figured out how scared I was?

I stepped into the swirl of the marketplace crowd, my muddy skirt brushing against tables full of dark clothes and dirty-looking vegetables. Something was different from the day before, something I couldn't quite identify.

No, I could—it was that, except for Bobo and me, there were no children here today. We were the only ones.

This is how the marketplace here would have looked for the past twelve years, before all of us kids came back, I thought. *Maybe yesterday everyone discovered how hard it is to shop with little children running around. Maybe they just hadn't known that before.*

I didn't think that was the reason.

How could I find out anything?

Listen, I told myself—the word that Edwy had kept hissing at me yesterday.

People around me were talking about the price of cassava root. They were grimly bargaining for packets, for extra portions of manioc flour. There was none of the cheery chatter I remembered from the Fredtown marketplace: *Oh, did you hear? Our little Nelly started walking yesterday! And now we're crawling around behind her, trying to keep her out of trouble! And You know what my little Lotu started calling his brother? Big Guy. It's so funny how he runs around the house calling, "Where Big Guy? Big Guy home from school yet?"*

Had all of the happy chatter in Fredtown been about us kids? And had the people in my hometown just lost the habit of happy chatter because they'd been without their kids for so long?

I got a little lost in the crowd, a little lost in my plans and fears. Was Bobo really safe on my back? Would he stay safe, even if I took a few risks to find Edwy?

I turned a corner, dodging the sharp edge of a table. I slammed into somebody's bony arm.

"Oh, sorry," I murmured. "Next time I'll watch where I'm going. I'll—"

Then I saw who I'd run into. I recognized the dress, the purse, the hat.

It was the mother.

CHAPTER
TWENTY-SEVEN

"**Rosi?**" **she said,** whirling on me, her eyes wide with horror. "And Bobo? Why are you here? Why did you disobey me? I told you to stay home!"

"I—," I began.

She wasn't listening. She grabbed my arm and dragged me away from the worst of the crowd. She dragged us to the edge of the marketplace, where the father was packing up apples.

Packing up early, just like yesterday, when I got scared.

What were the mother and the father afraid of?

"Look!" the mother exclaimed, shoving Bobo and me toward the father. Even though looking would do him no good. "Look who showed up! Our children! What are we going to do?"

She was trembling. Her voice shook too.

"Take them home immediately," the father said. "Don't wait for me. Hurry!"

"No," I said, pulling away from the mother. "I came here for a reason. I'm sorry I disobeyed, but I had to. Edwy . . . Edwy's missing, and I have to find him. He and I promised we'd look out for each other."

"Edwy Watanaboneset," Bobo chirped helpfully from my back.

The mother looked like we'd slapped her. She looked like she was going to slap us.

"Don't say that name here!" she said, frantically glancing around.

"Why not?" I asked. "Everybody should hear it. Everybody should know he's missing. Everybody should be looking for him right now!"

I felt sure that was what would have happened in Fredtown if anyone had ever gone missing—even without that scary word "kidnapping" attached to the disappearance. There would have been search parties assigned and precise search areas mapped out. Every possible hiding place would have been examined in no time flat.

That was what needed to happen here. That was how I could help Edwy.

If the adults weren't organizing anything like that, then the responsibility fell to me.

The mother was still staring at me in stunned horror. I edged away from her. With Bobo still on my back, I scrambled onto the nearest table. It was just boards laid across a pair of sawhorses, so it buckled beneath my feet. But the boards held and I dared to stand up, rising to my full height. Now Bobo and I towered above the crowd. I could see the tops of everyone's head. I could see everyone staring at me.

Good, I told myself. *That's what I wanted.*

"Everybody!" I cried out. "Listen! A boy has gone missing. Maybe he's even been kidnapped." I thought that was keeping the maid's confidence. I wasn't giving away that I'd talked to her. "It's Edwy Watanaboneset. He's twelve, the same age as me. Please help. Please, we've got to organize a search. . . ."

And that was when the first person punched me.

CHAPTER TWENTY-EIGHT

The punch knocked me backward. It landed in my gut, right at the edge of my ribs, and I doubled over, the weight of Bobo on my back throwing me off-balance.

Stay upright! My brain screamed at me. *Keep Bobo from falling! Keep him higher than the crowd, away from anyone who might hit him. . . .*

"Bobo, close your eyes!" I screamed. "Think about happy things and ignore . . ."

I didn't think he could hear me, because he was already screaming in my ear, a drawn-out howl of terror.

I'd failed. I hadn't protected him well enough. He was already traumatized.

Was there any way to protect him from whatever was going to happen next?

"Stop!" I wailed blindly to the crowd around me. "Stop! Hitting people isn't the way to solve anything! Let's just talk. . . ."

But my voice—my words—were useless. Hands grabbed at Bobo and me, pulling us down from the table, down into the dirt.

"Don't hurt Bobo!" I cried. "Be careful with Bobo!"

People surrounded us, pressing close, blocking out the sun overhead. A man screamed, "Did you hear her? Acting like she can tell us what to do? For one of *them*?"

It reminded me of what Edwy and I had overheard the night before, in the wasteland. Maybe this was even the very same man who'd complained, *Have you seen how those kids look at you?* Or the one who said, *They've got no respect.*

But I didn't understand what I'd done wrong. Was it standing on the table? Was it speaking Edwy's name aloud? Was it being a child, but already too old and too tall? Was it having green eyes? Something had unleashed a fury in all the grown-ups around me. Something had turned them into monsters who glared angrily at me.

"I'm just trying to help!" I protested, trying to rise up from the dirt while shielding Bobo. "Edwy needs—"

A shove knocked me down again. It was followed by somebody kicking me. And then I couldn't separate out who was hitting me. Fists pounded against my body.

"Stop!" I screamed again. "For Bobo's sake—"

Someone yanked Bobo away from me. One second he still had his hands clenched around my neck, his fingers intertwined as he held on for dear life. The next second he was gone, and I couldn't see who had him. I could only catch glimpses of the hands hitting me and the faces leering at me.

"Don't take Bobo!" I screamed. "Give him back!"

I didn't think. I couldn't. I waved my arms—shoving hands off me, struggling against the crowd. I'd balled up my hands into fists, and they connected with a jaw here, a gut there.

I was fighting back.

Turn the other cheek! screamed in my brain. *A gentle answer turneth away wrath! Nonviolence is the greatest force at the disposal of mankind!*

And yet my fists pounded against the bodies around me just as hard as fists pounded against mine.

"I want my brother back!" I screamed.

Nobody listened. A fist landed in my face, and it was such a big fist that I felt the pain all the way from my lower lip to the top of my nose. I felt something wet gushing down my cheek.

Blood.

They could kill me, I thought, stunned.

That couldn't happen, because I needed to be there for Bobo, needed to find Edwy. . . .

I swung my fists harder and faster. I struggled against the fists pounding me and managed to half sit up.

"Help!" I screamed. "Help! Somebody! Please . . ."

Why weren't the mother and the father coming to rescue me? Why hadn't the Freds known this might happen? How could they have sent me to a place like this?

I jerked my head back and forth, frantically looking for Bobo. He was nowhere in sight. All I could see were fists and hands and leering faces. There were so many of them. Had the fighting somehow extended to the entire marketplace? Were lots of people being beaten, not just me?

Everywhere I looked, I saw swinging arms, pounding fists.

And—over there—was that the glint of a knife?

Just then a blow landed against the side of my head. I felt my neck jarring from side to side, the pain reverberating.

I collapsed to the ground and everything went black.

CHAPTER TWENTY-NINE

I woke to darkness.

Is this how it happened for the father? I wondered. *When all the light in the world turned off for him?*

I found myself feeling for my arms, each hand grasping for the opposite elbow, the opposite forearm and hand. I flexed my leg muscles and feet. All my limbs were still there, but moving them shot pain through my entire body. I felt rips in my sleeves, gashes in my skin, dried blood everywhere.

I had never before had such serious wounds. I had never before had so much as a scratch that wasn't instantly tended to, that wasn't immediately dabbed with antiseptic and lovingly bandaged.

My heart ached with longing for the love and care of my Fred-parents, for the simplicity of life in Fredtown. Tears stung my eyes, but I couldn't blink them away. When I tried harder, I finally saw a hint of light.

It wasn't that my eyes had stopped working. It was that my eyelids were so painfully swollen that I could open them to only the barest of slits. And the light around me was so dim that at first it had seemed like darkness.

I forced myself to sit up. I forced my eyes open wider.

I was alone, on a cot. And I was in . . . a cage.

There were bars on three sides of me. The fourth side was a solid stone wall. The only section of the bars that looked like it might be a door was held firmly in place by a thick padlock.

I remembered Bobo looking at the caged-in, locked-down stores and thinking their bars were masks.

I remembered Bobo. I remembered that I'd lost him.

"Bobo!" I screamed. "Bobo!"

Nobody answered. Nobody came.

I remembered that we'd been trying to find Edwy. I remembered the maid saying that he'd been kidnapped.

"Edwy?" I called hopefully. Maybe he was being held nearby. Maybe he was just waiting for me to yell for him. That was the kind of thing he'd do. Maybe he'd figured out how to pick the lock on his cage. Maybe he was just hiding in the shadows to see if I would figure it out, too.

There was still no answer.

Even Edwy wouldn't be so cruel as to not answer when I sounded so desperate.

I stood up on trembling legs and struggled over to the nearest wall of bars. I wrapped my hands around two of the bars and tried to shake them loose.

The bars held firm, their ends embedded in the stone ceiling above me and the stone floor beneath my feet. I yanked at the padlock on the door, but it held fast. Clutching the bars or trying to open the door was as useless as clenching my hands into fists and hitting the people who hit me.

I fought just as hard as they did, I remembered, everything about the fight coming back to me.

Shame and guilt flooded over me. I had violated one of the most sacred principles the Freds had taught me: *You must never, ever, ever fight. Even if someone hits you, you don't hit back. You use your words and your wits and you settle disputes peaceably.*

I had had neither the words nor the wits to settle anything. I had fought, and I had lost Bobo. And now I was in a cage.

I collapsed to the floor and wept.

I was still weeping when I heard a voice: "Rosi? Rosi—is that you?"

I raised my head, forced my swollen eyes to open as wide as possible. I knew the voice didn't belong to Bobo or Edwy. It didn't belong to any child. It didn't belong to the mother or the father either.

But it was still a little familiar.

I heard footsteps and saw a figure approaching in the near-darkness. It wasn't until I caught a glimpse of slightly tilted eyes that I understood who had called my name:

It was the missionary from the mother's church.

CHAPTER
THIRTY

"**I'm here,**" I whispered. I raised my voice for what I really wanted to say. "Do you know—is Bobo all right? What happened to him?"

The missionary rushed toward my cage. He reached out and touched the padlock holding the door in place. Maybe he couldn't quite believe it was real either.

"Bobo is fine," he said in a cautious, soothing voice. "You don't have to worry about him or your parents. They all escaped safely. Without injury. I just saw them—in fact, your parents were the ones who sent me here. I got special permission. . . . Oh, I am so sorry."

I squinted up at him in confusion. The motion made my eyes and eyelids ache even more, the swollen skin bunching painfully together.

"*They* put me here?" I asked, heartbreak in my voice, no matter how hard I tried to hide it. "The parents? They think I belong in a . . . a cage?"

I thought of the mother slapping me, of the way she'd been mean to me from the very first. I thought of how she'd lied to the father about what color my eyes were. Had he found out the truth, and *this* was the result?

I thought again of how I'd hit and punched and kicked the people attacking me in the marketplace. How I'd fought. How I'd lost Bobo anyway.

Maybe I did belong in a cage.

"No, no, it was—" The missionary broke off. He ran his hand through his hair, which made it ripple like black silk. I let myself be distracted by that for an instant. His hair was completely different from mine.

It was easier to think about hair than about anything else right now.

And when I'd broken so many other important rules, what did it matter if I focused on someone's appearance?

The missionary sank down to the floor to sit beside me, just on the other side of the bars.

"A prisoner has the right to know why she is being imprisoned," he said. "So you can hear things now that you weren't allowed to know before."

Imprisoned? I thought.

I wanted to say that I already knew what I'd done wrong. But the words stuck in my throat. Nothing came out.

"First of all, I owe you an apology," the missionary said.

I raised my head and looked at him.

"This could get lost after you hear the rest, but I'm sorry for the way things went on Sunday," he said.

"Sunday?" I repeated, because after everything else that had happened, Sunday seemed a million years ago. But, depending on how long I'd been unconscious, it might have only been the day before.

"Yes. Yesterday," the missionary said, so at least I knew that much. "Yesterday morning at the church service . . . You have to understand. I minister to broken people who have known great sorrow and pain. For twelve years I'd hoped and prayed alongside them. Year after year, I had to comfort weeping couples who had tiny newborn babies ripped from their arms. After all that sorrow, can't you understand why, when God finally granted our prayers and you children returned, all we wanted to do was savor our joy? Rejoice in our miracle?"

I could almost see this, almost understand. But something perverse made me object.

"The mother, the father—the parents Bobo and I were sent back to—they never seemed happy to get *me* back," I said. It hurt to say that. To acknowledge that my own parents didn't seem to want me.

The missionary nodded in a way that accepted my words without agreeing.

"Your parents lost a baby when you were taken away," he said. "It's not that they expected you to still be a baby after twelve years, but . . . you and the other older children . . . you've already been shaped by the lives you lived apart from your parents. You've grown up very differently, into different people. More like . . . the people who raised you."

He meant the Freds. On Sunday I'd wanted to scream, *Freds aren't evil! Freds are good!*

Now I didn't even feel worthy to speak the name, Freds.

The missionary grimaced, but in a sympathetic way. It was almost a Fred expression.

"Jesus Himself would have been able to walk into that church and rejoice with the parents, but also comfort you children who felt bewildered and lost," he said. "I failed to do that. Until you stood up, I didn't even understand that I needed to. It had been so long since I'd been around children. . . . I'm sorry. I thought there would be time to explain that to you . . . before it came to this."

He glanced around, his gaze taking in the bars of my cage. Or prison. Maybe that's what it really was.

Somehow his apology—or confession—jarred loose one of my own.

"I know why I'm here," I admitted. "For fighting. It's understandable when little kids bite or hit or scratch, because they don't know any better. But I know it's wrong. I deserve . . ."

My throat closed again, and I couldn't finish. I might have managed to say, *to be in a cage. A prison.* But what if this man thought I'd deserved to lose Bobo? To never see him again?

I also wanted to say, *The mother slapped me—is she in a cage somewhere too?* But her slapping me hadn't caused my fighting. I was responsible for my own actions.

"Your Jesus is the one who said, *Turn the other cheek,* right?" I asked. "He'd hate me for what I did!"

"He would *forgive* you for what you did," the missionary said gently. "And that's if he thought what you did was wrong. Under the circumstances . . . Did you ever hear that Jesus also said, *I bring not peace, but a sword?*"

"He did?" I said. That had never once been mentioned in Fredtown.

"It's caused a lot of problems over the years," the missionary admitted. "I personally don't view it as a call to war. Just that sometimes God wants us to stir things up. And we're supposed to be wise enough to figure out when we need to be peaceable and abiding, and when we need to stand up and shout for change."

I latched onto the strange word he'd said.

"*War?*" I asked. "Why would you worry about that? There hasn't been a war in ages!"

The missionary froze.

"Is that what the Freds told you?" he asked in a strangely quiet voice. It made me think of ice that was about to crack.

"Yes, of course," I said confidently, using my school recitation tone. Coming home had been one challenge after another, but I could handle this. "Just as little children have to learn that hitting and lashing out is wrong and doesn't work, humanity as a whole did, too. A long time ago, before people were civilized, they had wars. Of course now we know that there are always other, better ways to work out conflicts. We know that war is much too terrible."

I couldn't remember any Fred telling me exactly when people had stopped fighting wars, but that was probably because it had been so long ago. Practically prehistory.

The missionary let his eyes close—a sign of weakness? prayer? Then he opened them again.

"Rosi, the last war ended only twelve years ago," he said. "The day you were born. You and Edwy. Two newborn babies miraculously saved from the heart of a war zone. . . ."

I couldn't deal quite yet with that strange and horrible concept—*war*—as something that had occurred during my lifetime. But I could inch toward it. The Freds had always said that Edwy and I were taken to Fredtown on the very day we were born. But they also said that newborns were generally considered too fragile to travel great distances. If Edwy and I had been born during a war, of course the risks of leaving us in place were greater than the risks of travel.

And if the war had ended, then the danger wasn't as great for the children younger than us. As babies, they could be left in their hometown, cared for by Freds, until they were a little stronger. They just had to be taken away eventually because . . . because . . .

Because their parents had once been in a war? Because they were still *capable* of war?

Something odd happened in my brain—something like double vision in my mind's eye. I could see the fighting I'd witnessed in the marketplace: the fists raining down on me, my screaming for Bobo, the glint of a knife slashing through the air. Was that what war was like?

And I could see the father's sightless eyes, his empty shirtsleeve; the mother's scarred, paralyzed face. I could see all the other disfigured and disabled adults in my hometown, the wasteland of burned houses.

Were all those signs of war, evidence of battles fought only a dozen years ago?

I remembered scrambling onto the table and screaming about Edwy's disappearance. I remembered swinging my own fists against the people hitting me.

"Did I just start another war?" I whispered.

CHAPTER
THIRTY-ONE

"**No,**" the missionary said, shaking his head emphatically. "No. You can't put that blame on yourself. The people who started the fighting . . . they were just looking for an opening. They had too much hate in their hearts to tolerate their former enemies getting their children back. And anyhow, Enforcers came and stopped everything. . . ."

He wouldn't quite meet my eye.

I remembered that back when there were wars, people died in battle.

"Bobo!" I wailed. "Are you *sure* he wasn't hurt? Did you see him for yourself? You're not just telling me what you think I want to hear, are you? Please tell me. . . ."

The missionary reached in through the bars and laid a hand on my shoulder.

"I promise you, Bobo is fine," he said. "Physically."

"But psychologically . . . ," I whimpered.

"I won't lie to you," the missionary said. "Of course he

was shaken up. And worried about you. But your parents are taking good care of him. I *did* see him. I helped your mother bandage the scrapes Bobo got from falling. He'll heal. Body and spirit."

I looked down at my own bloodied clothes.

"But people were beating us," I said. "And he's so small . . . how could he be fine? He had to have gotten hurt!"

The missionary's eyes darted to the side and back again.

"No," he said. "The people who attacked you left him alone. As soon as he was away from you."

"You mean he wasn't hurt because . . . because he doesn't have green eyes," I said.

For a long moment, the missionary only looked at me.

"You understand, then," he said.

"No!" I said, grabbing and shaking the bars again. "No, I don't understand anything! What does it matter what color anyone's eyes are? Why was that one of the first questions the father asked about me? Why did the mother lie and say my eyes were dark?"

The missionary put his hands against the bars between us.

"It shouldn't matter," he said. "It shouldn't. But . . . how much history do you know?"

"Nelson Mandela," I said. "Mahatma Gandhi. Martin Luther King . . ."

The missionary narrowed his eyes at me.

"Do you really know about those men?" he asked. "About the challenges they faced? The battles they fought? Or do you only know their noble words?"

"They *fought*?" I said in horror. "Even them?"

"Nonviolently," the missionary said quickly. "Although I think Nelson Mandela, in his early years . . . Never mind. Those three men really were notable for their nonviolence, as the Freds undoubtedly told you. But I don't know how you can fully understand their achievements unless you know the hatred they faced, the discrimination their people struggled against. . . . And in this country, your people never had a Mandela or a Martin Luther King or a Gandhi. This country only had the hatred."

"How does someone start hating someone else's *eyes*?" I asked. "Or the shape of their nose?"

"It was never really about eyes and noses," the missionary said. "I am an outsider, and people here will say to me, 'Oh, you can see by that person's face which side *he* was on. . . .' And I can't. There are people with noses that are both broad and long. There are people with eyes that are such a dark green that they're almost black. . . . Of course, I don't *want* to be able to see the differences."

That's what a Fred would say, I marveled.

"But—," I began.

"What people were really fighting over was history," the

missionary said. "Hundreds of years of history, hundreds of years of battles flaring up over one tribe of people having land or possessions another tribe wanted. Then it was people from one tribe remembering that the other tribe had killed their children, their parents, their friends . . . everyone they cared about. It was never letting go of a grudge, even after some people from the two tribes intermarried and the children inherited traits from both sides. Even then, one type of people decided another type of people had to be wiped off the face of the earth and tried to kill them all. . . ."

I shivered. This was too awful to think about.

"People aren't *types*," I said. "People are just people. Individuals."

"Yes," the missionary agreed. "Don't stop believing that. But you have to know now that some people don't think that way. You have to know that, to understand what happened today."

My mind skipped around, lighting on a fact I hadn't paid much attention to before.

"But my parents—the mother and the father—they have different-color eyes," I said. "And they both have injuries. How could that be?"

"In the war a dozen years ago," the missionary began slowly, "the dark-eyed people began killing the green-eyed people. The green-eyed people fought back; some dark-eyed people even fought on their behalf. To protect them. But then there was just killing and death. . . . Only the very strong and the very lucky survived."

Somehow I had not thought of the parents as strong. Or lucky.

And which side did my father fight on?

It was hard enough to think of anyone fighting. Then something worse occurred to me.

"But the children," I whimpered. "All the children who were here during that war, the ones who would have been only a little older than Edwy and me . . ."

The missionary winced.

"Some escaped," he said in a weak voice. "Their parents sent them far away, in the early days of the war, when it was still possible to leave. But then . . . the school was bombed. There was an epidemic, which doctors from outside could have treated, if it had been safe for them to come help. If sickness and warfare weren't such good friends. If the children hadn't already been so vulnerable. . . . The children who didn't die in the fighting died of the fevers. Died miserably . . ."

He didn't sound like a missionary. He sounded like a man lost in sorrow.

"But eventually the war *ended*," I said, clutching for something to be cheerful about.

"Only because the Freds came," the missionary said. "They stopped the war. And they started taking away every new baby that was born. They didn't think people could be trusted with their own children."

Something like hope sprang to life in my heart.

"Is that going to happen again?" I asked. "Will babies and children be taken away now because of what happened in the marketplace? Who did you say stopped the fighting this time—the 'Enforcers'? Is that just another name for Freds?"

"No," the missionary said, and now his face looked stern. "The Enforcers aren't Freds. They're . . . even crueler."

"Freds aren't cruel!" I objected.

A shadow crossed the missionary's face.

"I came to this town twelve years ago, right after the fighting stopped," he said. "Right after the first babies were taken away."

"Me and Edwy," I whispered. I remembered that I hadn't asked about Edwy yet, but I didn't think the missionary would answer me now. He looked like his mind was a million kilometers away—or maybe, more accurately, a dozen years in the past.

"People were already devastated by the death and destruction of war," he said. "But losing a baby— Babies are the future. Babies are hope. You probably look at this town as it is now and see only the things that are still broken. The scars and the missing limbs and the blinded eyes. The cracks in every foundation, the buildings that were never repaired. But I look around and see how far these people have come. They tried so hard to earn the right to get their children back. I was so proud of them. I thought God was blessing them. But now, sitting here with you, I see . . . exactly how much we made a deal with the devil."

I'd never heard that word—"devil"—before, but the way the missionary said it made fear crawl back into my heart.

"Sitting here with me makes you think that, because . . . ?" I prompted him.

He dodged my gaze for a moment, then grimaced and stared me straight in the eye.

"My faith tells me that forgiveness and redemption are always possible," he said. "But to get their children back, people had to agree that there would never again be second chances. They had to agree that anyone inciting violence would be imprisoned for the rest of their lives. And"—his voice dropped to a mournful whisper—"that's what the Enforcers believe you did."

CHAPTER
THIRTY-TWO

It took my mind a moment to catch up.

"They think I . . . ," I began numbly. "But I wasn't! I wasn't trying to get anyone to be violent! I wasn't asking to be hit! I wasn't planning to hit back! I was just trying to find Edwy!"

"I know, I know," the missionary said soothingly. He reached through the bars and patted my back. "It's not right. It's not fair. You weren't at fault. It's just that the Enforcers look at things so broadly. . . ."

"Then can't you tell them?" I asked. "The Enforcers? Can't I have, uh, an attorney to represent me, to prove my innocence?"

The missionary kept patting my back. I waited for him to say, *Of course. Of course that's how it will work. We'll get you out of here in no time.*

Instead, he sighed.

"The agreement we made to get you children back . . . ,"

he began. "Nobody thought it would affect a *child*. I guess people thought you would all be too peaceable, having been raised by Freds. Or just too young to cause anything. After twelve years, I think everyone forgot what children are like. We forgot that you would be just as human as adults. And that none of you would have learned to be cautious around enemies."

"In Fredtown none of us *had* enemies!" I protested. "We didn't know what enemies were!"

The missionary shook his head ruefully.

"I wish you'd never had to find out," he said. His eyes were glossy with unshed tears. "And I wish we adults had focused a little more on what would happen once you were home, and how your very presence could drive the sides apart again. Because people no longer had the common goal of getting their kids back. I guess we thought everyone would be too happy to do anything threatening right away. We thought there'd be a honeymoon period, a grace period. And . . . that there would be time to renegotiate the terms of the agreement before anything bad happened." He grimaced, and swallowed hard. "But the rules we agreed to— they're ironclad."

He raised his head and peered directly into my eyes.

"There's no appeals process," he said. "No attorneys. No hope. One accusation of inciting violence and the Enforcers can put a person away forever. They believe that is the only way to prevent more war."

A *deal with the devil,* I thought.

I thought I understood what the devil was.

"Well, *someone* has to explain," I said. "Can't you go to these Enforcers and tell them what I was really trying to do? Can't I talk to them?"

"No," the missionary said, shaking his head mournfully again. "That isn't the process. This is what the Enforcers have planned for you, for the rest of your life. You will at least be kept separate from the ones who fought against you, who were also imprisoned. And you will have meals brought to you three times a day, along with other necessities. Once a week you are allowed to have a visitor, but only from a spiritual adviser—that would be me, unless you request someone else. Lights will go out every night at eight p.m., and come back on at eight a.m. Twenty-four hours a day, you will be watched by a video camera."

He pointed toward a corner behind him, where two walls met the ceiling. Maybe if the light had been a little brighter— or if my eyes had been able to open a little wider—I might have been able to see the glint of a camera lens there.

"The Enforcers are also installing security cameras along the hallway that leads out of here," the missionary went on. His voice had settled into a neutral tone, as if these were details that didn't affect either of us. "They're putting in video cameras to watch every part of this community, to make sure that no battle starts up again. It's too late in the day right now, but I've been told that all those cameras will be up at first light tomorrow. And starting tomorrow, all of those cameras will have motion detection sensors. Even the one in here."

I barely heard him, because I was still stuck on an earlier detail: *Once a week you are allowed to have a visitor, but only from a spiritual advisor. . . .*

Was he saying I would never get to see Bobo again? Never get to see Edwy or Cana or Peki or Meki? My mind circled back again to the worst possibility, the one that would hurt the most: *Never get to see Bobo?*

"No," I whispered. "No. That's . . . unbearable."

As if on cue, the lights behind the missionary flickered.

"And that would be the warning that lights-out is in five minutes," he said. "If I don't leave now, the Enforcers will come and get me. Listen, I know this is awful for you, but you have to pay attention: I'm going to leave you with something that can save you. You will still have a few minutes of light after I'm gone—so start reading this tonight. It will provide comfort you probably can't even imagine right now. . . ."

He slipped something through the bars and into my hands. A book. I looked down, and though my sight blurred, I could read the letters in gold print on the black cover: Holy Bible.

"You think a *book* is going to save me?" I asked incredulously. "After everything you just told me?"

"Yes, yes, I promise you," the missionary said hurriedly. He was backing away from me now. "I'm sorry, so sorry, but really, just start reading. That's all you need. . . ."

He disappeared into the shadows and beyond my view. I heard his footsteps receding.

"No, please . . . ," I whimpered.

Nothing.

I threw the book he'd given me across the cage. Across my prison cell.

"A book?" I raged. "A *book* is all I have left to me?"

I waited, because maybe the missionary could still hear me; maybe he'd take pity on me and come back. I listened hard, but all I heard was the book hitting the floor with a thud and then a tiny echoing ping.

Edwy had been right back in Fredtown: Missionaries were horrible people.

Edwy . . . Bobo . . .

I drew in a breath, because I wasn't going to take this quietly—no way. If there was a video camera aimed at me twenty-four hours a day, then I would use that to make my appeal. I wasn't going to read any book; I would talk about why I deserved to get out of there until I convinced the

Enforcers—or whoever watched and listened through the video camera—to set me free.

If he'd really wanted to help me, why didn't the missionary suggest that? I wondered. *Instead of just giving me a book to read . . . or throw. . . .*

Belatedly, something struck me about how the Bible had hit the floor. That little extra ping at the end—what was that?

Books don't ping, I thought. *Not unless they have metal on them. Or in them.*

I'd only held on to the book for a moment before flinging it across the prison cell. But that was long enough to know there'd been no metal edging on its corners, no metal-tipped bookmark tucked inside.

Maybe . . . , I thought. *Maybe . . .*

I sat frozen, thinking hard. I waited the longest minutes of my life, until the lights suddenly blinked out. I waited until I was sitting in complete darkness.

And then I scurried over to the place where the book had landed. I felt around on the floor beside it. I felt under it. I felt between its thin, whispery pages.

And then, when my fingers finally brushed something slender and solid and spiky, I understood that the thing I'd barely dared to hope for was real:

The missionary hadn't just left me a Bible. He'd left me a Bible with a key hidden inside.

CHAPTER
THIRTY-THREE

Freedom, I thought.

I looked up at the dark corner of the room where the missionary had pointed out a video camera. During the instant when the book was flying through the air, was there any chance that the camera had captured a view of the key in the book? When the key landed, was the recording device strong enough to have heard the same ping that I did?

Nobody came. I could dare to hope that either the camera had caught nothing, or nobody had started watching and listening to the images and sounds it captured. I had time, but I didn't know how much.

I remembered what the missionary had told me, the information I'd barely paid attention to: *The Enforcers are also installing security cameras along the hallway that leads out of here. They're putting in video cameras to watch every part of this community, to make sure that no battle starts up again. It's too late in the day right now, but I've been told that all those cameras will be up at first light tomorrow.*

He'd said that so I would know I had to leave tonight. I couldn't hold on to the key for days, thinking and planning and figuring things out. Tonight was my only chance.

I tiptoed around the edges of my prison cell, feeling along the bars for the door and the padlock.

You have to do this quietly, I told myself. *You don't know how carefully they're listening.*

The padlock clanked against one of the bars when I finally reached it. The sound seemed to echo forever. If anyone was listening, there was no way they could miss hearing that.

Cover for it, I thought. *Make them think there's some other explanation besides me escaping. . . . Maybe just me being upset?*

"Awful, horrible, terrible bars and lock," I moaned. "I give up! There's no way out!"

Maybe I had learned something about being sneaky. The key slipped easily into the lock while I was moaning. I twisted it and felt the lock click open even as I cried *I give up!* I pushed the door open as I finished *There's no way out!*

I stood in the doorway of my unlocked prison cell. Somehow the air hitting my face felt cooler and fresher now.

But probably this was just the easy part of escaping.

Don't make any mistakes, I told myself. *Pretend . . . pretend this is a school assignment, and you want to get one hundred percent. A perfect grade.*

Was there anything I needed to think of before I stepped out into the hall?

That Bible, I thought. *You can't leave it or the key behind, or someone will figure out that the missionary helped you get out. You don't want to get him in trouble.*

Weaving slightly, I retraced my steps in the darkness and picked up the book. I tucked it into my dress and made sure my belt held it in place before I headed back to the doorway. Then I eased the key out of the lock and dropped it into one of my pockets. I stopped to listen—no sound, anywhere. The silence was as thick and vast around me as the darkness.

Doesn't mean you're safe, I told myself. *Doesn't mean you can take any chances.*

I tiptoed toward the hallway where I'd seen the missionary leave. But my sense of direction was off—I bumped into a wall and scraped my chin on solid rock.

What's another scrape when you're already so beaten up? I thought. *You've been beaten—but not defeated.*

This near-rhyme amused me, and carried me through another series of steps forward. This time I had the sense to brush my fingers along the stone to keep myself from running into the wall again.

Five steps. Ten. Twenty. Had I missed a door in all this

darkness? Was there nothing *but* darkness left in the world?

Unbidden, the thought came back of all those fists raining down on me, all the punches and kicks. How could people who didn't even know me hate me so much for things that had happened before I was born?

How could I survive outside this prison when there were so many people who hated me for no good reason?

That thought made me falter. But the Bible jabbed against my stomach, reminding me that the missionary had taken risks to help me. That my parents had sent him to me. The least I could do was help myself.

I decided I would think about how to survive after I got out of this hallway.

I'm not sure how far I had gone—thirty steps? forty? a hundred?—when I saw the first glimmer of light both ahead and above me. Was the floor sloping upward?

A few steps more and I could see: I was in a tunnel, and the tunnel was about to come to an end. Evidently, my prison cage had been underground.

I tiptoed closer to the light and the tunnel's end, and I saw why this arrangement made sense: That meant there was only one exit to guard.

And this exit *was* guarded: A man sat at a desk, blocking the way out. I still stood in darkness, but I could see the profile of the man's head. It was framed in the light glowing from a lamp on his desk. And, seeing that, I understood why it wouldn't do me any good to appeal to the Enforcers, why they wouldn't even listen to my explanations.

The man sitting at the desk was the whiskery-faced man who'd been so mean to me on the plane.

He'd come back.

CHAPTER THIRTY-FOUR

I felt hopeless all the way down to my toes. There was no way I could get past that man. No way he'd be kind enough to just let me go.

I heard footsteps coming from the other side of the man's desk. Was it someone planning to come down into the cave? Would I have to run all the way back to the cage to hide? And if I did that, would I ever make it this far again?

A chin came into my range of vision; apparently, a second man had stepped up alongside the desk.

Is that—?

I couldn't see well enough to tell who it was until I heard the man's voice.

"I came back to tell you . . . the Lord would forgive even someone like you," the voice said.

It was the missionary.

"Go away," the man at the desk snarled.

He looked back down at papers strewn across his desk,

and the missionary stretched his neck forward, gazing down toward me. I could see his whole face. Would it help if he could see me, too?

I thrust my hand into the lit-up area in front of me. I *waved* at the missionary, and hoped against hope that the whiskery Enforcer wouldn't choose that moment to glance back too.

The missionary gave a slight nod, as if he'd seen me. What was I supposed to do next?

All I could think to do was yank my hand back out of the light. The missionary didn't glance my way again.

"What I say is true," the missionary told the whiskery man. "I swear. Want me to tell you the story of a jailer in the Bible? Of course, it took an earthquake to get him to believe. I've always kind of pictured the rocks of his prison as being a lot like the rocks hanging right over your head."

Now the whiskery man glanced up. And then, before I had a chance to move, he glanced back toward me.

You're completely in darkness again, I told myself. *You got your hand back out of the light in time. He can't see you! You're safe!*

"Oh, sorry—am I making you nervous?" the missionary asked, and the whiskery man snapped his attention back that way. "I didn't mean to. Look, if you want, I can help you move your desk so it's not right *under* those rocks."

And then, without waiting for the man to say yes or no, the missionary grabbed one side of the desk and yanked it toward him.

I saw what he was trying to do before it happened. The lamp on the desk tilted over and plummeted to the ground. It hit with a sound of breaking glass and shattering lightbulbs. I dared to hope for total darkness afterward, but there was still a dim glow coming from overhead, outside the tunnel. Was it that same bright moon that had guided Edwy and me the night before? Or some other lamp mounted in the rock over the guard's head?

I didn't have time even to guess. Because the guard stepped out from behind the desk and started swinging fists at the missionary.

"I told you to go away!" the guard screamed. "Now look what you've done!"

"Sorry, sorry—but if you punch me, aren't you violating the code you're sworn to uphold as an Enforcer?" the missionary asked, dancing away from the guard.

"Enforcers are allowed to use violence!" the guard yelled back at him. "We're the only ones who are!"

I hoped they kept screaming, because I needed noise to cover the sound of my running feet. I launched myself up the last few meters of the sloping tunnel.

Keep fighting, I thought, as if I could control the

movements of the guard and the missionary. *Keep screaming, keep moving farther from the desk.* . . .

I reached the opening of the tunnel just as the guard grabbed the missionary by the scruff of his neck and threw him into the darkness.

"And don't come back!" the guard hollered. "Ever! I just put an electronic tracker on you! Your movements will be monitored from now on!"

Was that true or just a bluff? Was that even possible?

All that fell out of my mind. Because I could see the guard shift his weight, ready to turn back to the desk, back toward *me*. Unless I moved instantly, I'd be in full view of the guard in mere seconds.

I couldn't tell what lay just beyond the opening of the tunnel. For all I knew, maybe I'd be in full view of the guard no matter which way I turned. But he would definitely see me if I stayed in the tunnel.

I squeezed through the space between the rock of the tunnel opening and the shoved-aside desk. I held my breath and leaped over the broken lamp and its broken glass. As soon as I landed, I whirled off to the side. I pressed against the side of a dark building and burrowed into the shadows lurking there.

The only light *was* from the moon. The overhang of this building's roof kept me out of its glare.

The guard walked toward me, but he was looking down, toward the lamp. He swore under his breath as he turned away. And then I heard him slide out a drawer. He spoke into some sort of intercom or walkie-talkie.

"Yeah, bring me a pack of lightbulbs as soon as you can get someone over here," he growled. "And put missionaries on the list of people who aren't allowed to see prisoners."

I eased back farther into the shadows, farther from him. My heart pounded furiously in my chest. I'd gotten away. Thanks to the missionary, I'd escaped the prison.

But if his every move was being monitored now, I couldn't expect any more help from him. I just had to hope that he would stay safe. It would be too dangerous to try to follow him home or to hide out at his church.

So what was I supposed to do now? Where could I possibly go?

CHAPTER THIRTY-FIVE

To Bobo, I thought, his name thrumming inside me just as it had ever since I'd awakened in the prison cell.

Wherever I went, whatever I did, whatever safety I managed to find, I couldn't leave Bobo behind. I couldn't let him think I'd abandoned him.

That told me where I had to go first. I could figure out the rest from there.

I edged silently along the dark building, still hidden in the shadows. My eyes were starting to adjust to the darkness. I could make out an expanse of uneven cobblestones; I could make out rows of abandoned, tipped-over sawhorses. And suddenly I knew where I was, what the prison faced: the marketplace.

It was deserted now, desolate in the moonlight. My feet skidded on something dark and wet.

Blood? I thought in horror. *Was there so much blood left behind this afternoon that no one could wash it away? Did anyone even try?*

I had to get Bobo away from this horrible town. The two

of us needed to run away—back to Fredtown, if we could. To anywhere else that was safe, if Fredtown wasn't possible.

There. I had a plan.

I reached the edge of the building with its wonderful low shadow-throwing roof. I glanced cautiously from side to side before leaping into the shadows alongside the next building. The marketplace looked different by moonlight, but I thought I was heading toward the creek.

I heard footsteps behind me.

Take off running and risk being heard? I wondered. *Or just keep hiding and hope they don't come close?*

My legs decided for me. They were trembling so much, I didn't trust them to hold me up if I tried to run. I pressed my body as tightly as I could against the building.

"Here. The lightbulbs you asked for," a voice said behind me. "Now I'm back to patrol."

"Oh, stay and have a drink with me." This was the voice of the whiskered man back at the desk. "This is a town of rabbits. Did you see how they scattered when we showed up this afternoon? No one's going to break our new curfew tonight."

A new light appeared, menacingly bright. The lamp on the whiskery man's desk was working again. Was the glow strong enough to expose me?

I directed my thoughts at the guard and the patroller: *Don't look this way. Don't come over and walk along this building. . . .*

By craning my neck, I could see the shadows of the guard and the patroller, stretching across the cobblestones. The shadows were so long, they looked like monsters.

"Oh, but if I do catch anyone breaking curfew, remember, I'm allowed to shoot them," the patroller said. "Gotta love Agreement 5062!"

Agreement 5062? I thought. My brain ached. My heart did too. The paper I'd found by Edwy's seat on the plane had mentioned Agreement 5062. But it hadn't said anything about shooting people. I would have remembered that.

Unless . . . was that in the section of the page that was torn off? I wondered in horror.

"You *wanted* these people to mess up?" the guard asked the patroller. "You wanted to have to come back here?"

"Oh, you know," the patroller said, chuckling. "I do love hunting rabbits."

I heard a clicking sound, and the patroller's shadow held something long and thin up to his shoulder. He grunted: "Pow!"

Is that a gun? I wondered. I told myself he was just showing off. *But when he talks about hunting rabbits, does he really mean people? Would he really shoot them? Actual people? He'd hurt someone just for being out at night?*

I couldn't stay here. And I couldn't leave Bobo in this horrible town for an instant longer than necessary.

Now my legs wanted to run and run and run—to never stop running. But I didn't. It took all the self-control the

Freds had ever taught me to make my next movements slow and steady, an easing away from the guard and the patroller, rather than a frantic fleeing.

Go, go, go, go! sounded in my brain, even as my feet slid forward one *sloooowww* step at a time.

I reached the edge of the building and crawled to the edge of the next.

It was like this all the way to the creek, and then I had to creep from tree to tree to tree.

This was the longest night of my life, and it had barely even begun.

Peeking down along streets I passed, I saw three more patrollers, guns cocked at their shoulders as they turned and aimed at every noise. Three times I had to freeze behind trees and wait until the patrollers passed by.

I reached the turnoff for Edwy's street and wondered where he was. Had his family somehow gotten him back, even without my help? Which would be worse, being trapped by kidnappers or being out here in the darkness, cowering like a rabbit, just waiting for one of those patrollers to find me?

I told myself that being held by kidnappers was worse. Because I had choices and control—at least for now—and Edwy didn't.

I kept going.

I reached the turnoff for my own street, and I told myself

the rest of the route would be no different than it had been the night before.

But the night before, I'd been afraid only of the men chasing after Edwy. There hadn't been patrollers out with guns, planning to shoot anyone they saw.

And the night before, I'd left the door unlocked. And, even then I'd accidentally awakened the father.

I'll go in through a window this time, I told myself. *I'll be so quiet, nobody will hear me. I'll just scoop up Bobo in my arms and sneak back out. . . .*

The street seemed endless as I darted from house to house, hiding in shadows. My muscles ached from tiptoeing—or maybe it was from being beaten earlier in the day. The pain blended together. Every step hurt.

The missionary believed I could get away, I told myself. *Otherwise, he wouldn't have taken a chance on giving me a key. Or annoying the guard.*

Somehow this helped. I spared a thought—or maybe it was a prayer—for him. I hoped he made it home safely too.

I didn't quite understand why he had risked his life to rescue me.

He almost acted like a Fred, I thought. *Better than a Fred, even.*

Did the Freds understand what they were sending us back to? They'd stopped a war a dozen years ago—didn't they understand that one could start again? That having us children back could *make* these townspeople start it again?

There were rules, I thought. *Agreements. They didn't want to send us home, but they thought they had to. Freds believe in following rules.*

I wasn't sure I did anymore. Not every time. Not if rules put children in harm's way.

Was this what Edwy meant back on the plane when he wouldn't help me settle the other children down? I wondered. *Is that all Edwy ever believed? Did he think the rules keeping us ignorant were dangerous too?*

My mind was carrying me farther than my feet. I made myself concentrate on putting one foot in front of the other, inching from one shadow to the next. All I could think about was getting to Bobo.

Finally I reached the front of the parents' house and slipped around the side. I was in luck—the window to the room where Bobo slept was open. I couldn't see inside, but it was late now—it felt like it had taken me hours to walk from the marketplace. Of course, Bobo would already be in bed.

I eased the screen away from the window and slid one leg over the windowsill, then the other.

Immediately, hands grabbed me.

CHAPTER
THIRTY-SIX

"Let me go!" I tried to scream. But one of the hands that held me in place wrapped itself over my mouth, muffling my words.

"No, no, Rosi, it's us!" a voice hissed in my ear.

It was the mother's voice. It was her and the father holding me.

They began dragging me out of the room, and I let them. We had to have awakened Bobo, and I didn't want him to see when they started slapping and scolding me. But as we reached the other room, they didn't do any of that.

Instead, they hugged me.

"You're safe! Thank God you're safe!" the mother moaned.

"We thought we'd never see you again," the father wailed.

I pulled back. I peered into their tear-stained faces.

"You never acted like you cared this much about me before," I muttered, too stunned to hold back the truth.

"You weren't what we expected," the mother said. Maybe she'd been stunned into speaking the truth too. "You seemed so much like a Fred. Not anything like us. But today we understood. . . ."

Had my fighting back made them think I was more like them than like the Freds?

The father shook his head, as if he knew what I was thinking.

"Before, we kept thinking about how we'd lost your childhood," the father said. "Today, we could have lost *you*."

I wasn't buying it. I narrowed my eyes at the mother.

"You *slapped* me," I said.

"Just as my mother used to slap me when I was a smart-mouthed teen," the mother said. "When I didn't show her proper respect."

And how does that make it right? I wanted to protest. *Just because you got hurt, I have to be hurt too?*

But the mother was already lowering her eyes, already admitting, "Maybe she shouldn't have done that. Maybe I shouldn't have either. I didn't know how else to be a mother."

Did that make sense? Was that another reason the Freds had taken us away?

The father still had his arm around my shoulder, hugging me against his warped barrel of a chest as though I was his most precious possession.

"My eyes are actually green," I told him, because I couldn't let myself relax into the hug if it wasn't meant for the real me, the real green-eyed Rosi. The one who started people fighting. The one who fought back.

The father kept hugging me.

"I know," he said. "I figured that out on the first day. Dark eyes usually don't go with your nose shape. And I could tell your mother was lying."

"But—why?" I asked. "Why would she do that? I thought that meant you hated people like me!"

"*He's* not like that," the mother whispered. "I have green eyes too. Why would he have married me if he hated my eyes?" There was almost pride in her voice. Then it turned sad again. "But . . . I didn't want him to worry. In the last war, most of the people who died looked like you and me."

I winced, thinking again of the fists beating me in the marketplace. Would I ever be able to forget the horror of that moment?

To my surprise, I thought of something good about the parents and their differing eye color.

"He protected you, didn't he?" I asked the mother, remembering what the missionary had told me. "In the last war, the father was one of the dark-eyed people who tried to keep a green-eyed person safe. . . . He tried to keep *you* safe."

I was just guessing, but somehow I felt almost certain about this.

The mother lifted her head high and nodded.

"He did," she said, and she definitely sounded proud now. "And he'll protect you. . . ."

The father's face stayed dark and forbidding.

"Now that you understand the danger, we can work together to keep you safe," the father said. "We can hide you."

"And you'll stay where you're supposed to," the mother added sternly. Her shoulders slumped again.

I looked down at the rug that hid the hollowed-out space under the floor. Was that what they meant? What was the difference between being locked in a prison cell the rest of my life and hiding there?

The prison cell had actually had more space.

Just pretend to go along with this, I told myself. *Wait until they go to bed, then grab Bobo and leave.*

But I remembered the tone in my father's voice when he'd shown me the hiding place. He'd trusted me. I remembered the way the mother had held Bobo, how she'd buried her face in his hair. She loved him. Maybe she even loved me.

"No," I said, and I was surprised by the ringing authority in my voice. "I can't just hide. I have to go away. With Bobo. I'll take him someplace safe. Someplace we can grow up without fear or fighting."

"Don't you see—the world just isn't like that!" the mother said.

"But shouldn't it be?" I asked. "Where's the next town? Where's the nearest safe place? I mean, really—you two could come too!"

Tears began rolling down the mother's face.

"No, we couldn't," the father said gruffly.

"You might as well tell her," the mother said, her voice choked.

"In the war twelve years ago . . . the way we fought back . . . ," the father began. "We weren't just victims."

"We had to defend ourselves!" the mother interrupted. "We didn't want to die!"

The father let out a heavy sigh and shook his head.

"We were branded war criminals," he said. "We aren't allowed to leave."

Even a day ago, I wouldn't have been able to understand what they were talking about. But now I just kept staring into my parents' eyes.

"I—I fought back today too," I whispered. "I . . . hit, and I punched and I kicked. . . ."

"We did worse," the father said simply.

Did he mean that they'd maimed other people like they were maimed?

Did he mean that they'd *killed* them?

Just then, several loud booms sounded outside, then a *rat-a-tat-tat* that sent chills down my spine.

"Gunfire," the mother whispered, stiffening. "It's starting all over again."

"Oh no," I moaned. "What if the missionary's still out there? Pastor Dan? The patrols . . . I heard they were going to shoot anyone out after curfew. . . ."

"Those shots are coming from a different part of town," the father assured me. "But . . ."

Footsteps sounded from Bobo's room, and a second later he appeared in the doorway.

"I'm scared," he wailed, his fists held tight and terrified against his face. "Make that noise stop!"

And then he launched himself at me and clutched my legs for dear life.

I reached down and swept him up into my arms. I patted his back.

"There, there," I murmured as he wept onto my shoulder. "Someone must have forgotten . . . forgotten that nobody should play such loud games at night."

I shot a defiant look over Bobo's shoulder at the mother, because I was sure she would reach for him, sure she would try to take him from my arms and hug and comfort him herself.

But she didn't. She took a step back, giving me room. She

and the father both had tears streaming down their faces.

"We can't . . . ," the father began in a choked voice. His face twisted. "We can't make our children live like this."

"You . . . you do have to take Bobo someplace safe, Rosi," the mother whispered. "Even if it means we never see you again. Even if . . ."

She broke off, because the father clutched her arm and shook his head, as if he'd just heard something we all needed to pay attention to. And then I heard it too: footsteps. Outside.

Then someone knocked at the door.

CHAPTER THIRTY-SEVEN

Still clutching Bobo, I scrambled for the rug hiding the hole in the floor. The father began helping me pull the rug aside and lift the floorboard. The mother raced for the door, calling, in a voice that trembled, "Wait, just wait, this latch is so tricky. . . ."

Faintly, I heard a woman's voice call back from outside, "No, please, be quick. . . ."

The mother opened the door a crack, and then all the way.

"What are you doing?" I cried. We didn't even have the floorboard fully off the hiding place yet; there was no time to slip down out of sight.

"It's okay, it's okay," the mother called over her shoulder, even as someone in a hooded cape stepped into the house.

The mother shut the door behind her, and the intruder dropped the hood of her cape.

It was the maid from Edwy's house.

"Our neighbor, Drusa," the mother said, a helpless tone in her voice. I wasn't sure if she was telling the father or telling me. "From across the street."

I started to say, *Oh, we've met.* I might have even added the polite Fred-approved *How nice to see you again.* But the maid, Drusa, wasn't waiting for pleasantries. She gripped the mother's arm.

"I saw your daughter come back," she said. "I was watching. You're going to have to send her away before anyone finds her here. I'm just asking . . . take my daughter too."

And then, from the folds of her cape, she eased out a little girl who'd been hiding there.

It was Cana.

Cana's mother has only had her home for three days and she already wants to get rid of her? I thought. *Cana? The sweetest child ever?*

Drusa placed her hands on Cana's shoulders, and I understood.

No, it's killing this woman to send Cana away, I thought. *But she thinks she has to do this for Cana's sake.*

"That's fine," I said, trying to keep my voice light. "Cana and I are friends, aren't we, Cana?"

Cana's knowing eyes seemed to take in the tears still streaming down Bobo's cheeks, the dark, gaping hole in our floor, the tense expressions on all the grown-ups' faces. But she nodded.

"It's too much to ask," the father said. "Adding another child to take care of puts Rosi in more danger. And Bobo, too."

I glanced quickly at Bobo and then Cana—what if they understood that the father was calling Cana dangerous?

Cana's expression hardened; Bobo's lower lip trembled. But it had already been trembling.

"In exchange, I'll tell you the best place for your daughter to go," Drusa said. "I'll tell you where the Watanabonesets probably sent their son to be safe."

"What?" I exploded. "You mean Edwy? You told me Edwy was kidnapped! Were you lying? If I hadn't thought Edwy was in danger, I wouldn't have stood up in the market-place, I wouldn't have—"

Drusa just gave me an even stare.

"I don't know *what* happened to Edwy," she said. "The Watanabonesets told me to say he was kidnapped. And they were listening from behind the door, so I couldn't say anything else without being fired. They were acting upset, but everybody's been upset and worried ever since all of you children got home."

"We forgot how much worse it is to be in danger when our children are in danger too," the mother said softly. "Our innocent children."

She was gazing down at Bobo. The innocent one. The favorite. Then her eyes met mine, and they seemed to go a little dead. But I saw this differently now—now that I'd faced danger myself and failed to protect Bobo. My memories of all her scowling shifted. All those times she seemed so mad at me, had she really just been scared? And she couldn't hide it from me the same way she hid it from Bobo?

I couldn't think about any of that right now.

"How can you not even know if Edwy was kidnapped or sent to safety?" I fumed at Drusa, "Why would his parents lie? Why—?"

"You don't know what it's like in this town," Drusa snapped back at me. "Nobody ever knows what's true and what's false. It's too dangerous. Lies are the only protection *anyone* has. And lies don't work against bullets when madmen roam the streets with guns."

I thought about the gunfire we'd heard, off in the distance. I thought about how I was going to have to go back out into the dark night, into that danger.

"My daughter asks questions," Drusa said. She'd evidently given up on trying to explain this town to me. "Cana *thinks*. She expects the world to be nice to her. And . . . I want her to grow up like that. Not like I did, trusting no one. Scared of everything. Believing nothing." She reached into a pocket and pulled out a thin sheet of paper. "I have a map. I copied it from one I found on Mr. Watanaboneset's desk. Regardless of what actually happened to Edwy, if Mr.

Watanaboneset thought he should send his son away to keep him safe, I want that for my daughter, too."

She handed me the map and I took it with numb fingers. I tucked it into my pocket, beside the key I'd found in the missionary's Bible.

"We'll bundle up food for you to take," the mother said, wringing her hands. "And maybe a change of clothes . . . You won't be able to carry much. It won't take any time at all to pack."

She'd barely said the word "pack" when the door smashed open, not even swinging on its hinges but falling flat to the floor. If any of us had been standing in front of it, we would have been crushed. I couldn't make sense of the motion— there'd been so much noise. Had the hinges just exploded? On their own?

In the next instant, a man with a gun appeared in the doorway.

An Enforcer.

CHAPTER
THIRTY-EIGHT

Did he just shoot *the door open?* I wondered numbly. *Kick it down?*

Either way, he had so much power.

"You're hiding a fugitive!" he screamed.

He meant me. There was no avoiding it: He was going to recapture me. And he was going to punish my parents because he'd found me here. Maybe he'd even punish Drusa and Cana and Bobo.

"No!" I said. "None of them are responsible for me being here! I came on my own. Arrest me, but don't—"

"Arrest you?" the Enforcer cried in a horrible, mocking voice. "You're an escapee! I can do anything I want!"

And then he aimed his gun at me.

I couldn't breathe. I couldn't move. I couldn't see anything but that gun.

That's why I missed seeing my mother and Drusa fling themselves at the Enforcer. I only saw them smash into him, knocking the gun to the side. It went off, a bullet tearing through the roof.

These women aren't rabbits, I thought. *This is how mothers protect their young.*

"What's happening? Who's hit?" my father wailed, and my heart ached for him that he couldn't see, he didn't know.

"We're all fine," I tried to tell him, but at the same time my mother cried "Help us hold him down!"

My father leaped toward them. Bobo and Cana clutched my legs, making it impossible for me to move. Were the children screaming? Were the adults? Was I? All the noise jumbled together. Then I could make out Bobo's voice.

"I don't like this game!" he protested. "I don't want to play! Make it stop!"

He still thought this was make-believe. He thought none of this was real. It was like his mind was protecting him from understanding what he'd seen.

Just then my parents and Drusa pulled back from the Enforcer. My mother moaned, "Ohhhh . . . ," and Drusa began repeating, "So it's true. So it's true. It was true all along. . . ."

I couldn't see what they were talking about, but I could tell that the Enforcer had stopped moving. Bobo and Cana were still clutching my legs, and Bobo had his face buried in my skirt. But it was unbearable not to know what the women were looking at, unbearable not to know what my father had touched before his hands jerked away from the Enforcer's face. It was unbearable not to know what had happened. I inched forward, ready to push Bobo and Cana back if I saw anything that they shouldn't.

But Bobo got ahead of me. He thought the game was over; he thought the danger had been imaginary all along. He tiptoed close to the Enforcer, his mouth agape. He wore his fascinated expression, his "I'm about to ask questions" look. He stared at the place where the Enforcer's face had been. Now it seemed to be covered by glossy black scales. And antennae. And a horned forehead.

"Wow," Bobo breathed. In awe. "Is that what everyone looks like under their skin? Does everyone have a face like a beetle underneath their regular face? I want to see *my* beetle face. Can you get a mirror?"

He began tugging at the skin on his jaw, practically grunting with the effort.

Our father put his hand against Bobo's face, stopping him.

"You don't have a face like that," our father said. "Humans just have one face. The only people with beetle faces underneath are . . ."

Our mother finished for him in a whisper: "People from another planet."

CHAPTER
THIRTY-NINE

"**What?**" I said. "*What?*"

My mind was so jumbled.

This can't be echoed in my brain, swirling around every thought. *I'm just imagining this. Because of the trauma of this whole day, the trauma of every day since we came home . . . This can't be true, because I've never encountered anything like this before, never even thought it was possible. . . .*

Except maybe I had.

My mind jumped to the words I'd seen carved into Edwy's airplane seat: "These people aren't real either." I'd forgotten about those words, dismissed them entirely once Edwy said he wasn't talking about our real parents. I'd pretty much forgotten about the Enforcers too after I left the plane, before they became my jailers. But I should have been paying more attention. There were lots of things I should have noticed before it was too late.

These people aren't real either.

Either.

My mind couldn't seem to grasp anything. The three adults—the three *human* adults—acted just as befuddled. My parents were sprawled sideways, motionless, as if they'd slipped into shock. Drusa kept murmuring, "So it's true. It's true. I always thought those were just rumors. Made-up stories. Lies . . ."

Cana and Bobo were still young enough that they believed in the tooth fairy. Unicorns. Magic. Things that adults and kids my age considered impossible.

So somehow they didn't seem as surprised.

"Oh, he's a spaceman," Bobo said, nodding as if everything made sense to him now. "Or a spacewoman. Whatever. He's from a planet where people looks like beetles. So the fake human face—is that kind of like his space helmet?"

"Space people can't breathe without their space helmets on," Cana said in her wise little voice.

She darted toward the Enforcer and began tugging on the part of his face that had fallen away. Maybe she hit some kind of latch or lever, because suddenly the man's human face closed up again, hiding everything that resembled a beetle— the antennae, the horns, the shiny scales. His face seemed to be made of normal human skin again, but he was scowling, with ridges in his forehead, frown lines around his mouth. Now he looked human again. Human, but no less terrifying.

His whole body convulsed. I saw what Cana had figured out: The man had stopped breathing when his human face was off.

Was he still alive? Was the convulsing a sign that he was able to breathe again? Or a sign that he was dying?

The Enforcer's motion seemed to shake my parents out of their shock.

"Oh! We have to make sure—," my mother began.

"That he gets back to his friends for help," I said quickly, shooting a glance at Cana and Bobo. I couldn't let them understand. I wasn't even sure that I understood. But I was pretty sure my mother meant that this Enforcer had to die. Before he killed all of us. Or told someone else to.

"I'll take care of him," my father said heavily. "I'll—" He turned his head toward Bobo and softened his voice. "I'll take him to friends."

Numbly, I watched my father pull the spaceman/ Enforcer out into the street. I watched my mother and Drusa start to lift the broken door and place it back over the empty, gaping doorway, hiding our living room from the outside world once again. Just before they fit the splintered wood into the frame, I slid away from Cana's grip and darted after my father. I barely managed to squeeze past the door and out into the darkness.

"Wait!" I called after my father. "It's not safe! The

Enforcers who are out on patrol—they're shooting people on sight—"

"I'm not going far," my father whispered to me. He hesitated, crouched down, his hands under the spaceman/Enforcer's armpits. "There are people who would pay good money to have one of these Enforcers as a prisoner. So they can find out his secrets."

"But it's *dangerous* out here," I whispered. "You can't see—"

"Which means I'm safer in the dark than you are," he whispered back. "It's what I'm used to, anyway."

He began tugging on the spaceman's unconscious body, dragging it away from me and our house.

"Go back and take care of Bobo," my father said. "He needs you."

It was true: Bobo did need me. Bobo could easily be traumatized by what he'd just witnessed if he didn't get the right debriefing.

But so could I. I *had* been traumatized. My mind was still reeling.

These people aren't real either . . . either . . . either . . .

The words that Edwy had carved into the airplane seat still echoed in my brain. Now that I understood how unreal—or surreal—the Enforcers really were, Edwy's words sent me back to another disturbing memory: the moment when Edwy and I had stopped being friends back in Fredtown. It was after Edwy had started lying, constantly coming up with mischievous little stories that made me distrust anything he told me. I'd been stung too many times by his pranks—he dyed the tips of my hair orange with Kool-Aid once; another time he threw a shaving-cream pie in my face.

Then he came to me with a story about how he suspected something was really wrong with the Freds. His Fred-parents didn't trust him anymore either, so they were always on guard around him. But he knew that Fred-mama and Fred-daddy trusted me. He wanted me to tug hard on one of their faces—really, really hard. He told me something strange might happen—something we could figure out together. He didn't understand it, but he thought he'd seen something once when his Fred-parents didn't know he was looking. He said he needed my help.

You mean, you want me to get in as much trouble as you're always in, I'd told him.

Just talking to Edwy had made me uncomfortable after that. I hadn't wanted to know anything he'd guessed. I hadn't wanted to know anything bad or dangerous or suspicious about the Freds.

I loved them.

But now I stared into my real father's face—my real, blind, scarred, maimed father's face—and I wanted to see and know everything. I *had* to, if I ever had any hope of getting to safety with Bobo and Cana.

"This Enforcer—and all the others, too?—they're from another planet," I began, my voice barely audible. Only a blind man accustomed to listening for the smallest of sounds could have heard me. "But . . . the Freds weren't human, either. Were they?"

My father winced, frozen in the act of dragging an alien.

"That's the only theory I ever heard that made any sense," he said. "We never knew for sure—there's not much we know about anything. After the war, nobody wanted to talk about any of it. Everyone shunned our town. None of us adults could leave. No one ever came here except that one missionary. And . . ."

"And Freds," I whispered. "And now . . . Enforcers."

My father barely nodded.

"Those Enforcers are like the soldiers that roamed the street during the war," he said. "I understand *them*. They use weapons and threaten to kill anyone who doesn't obey. But how did the Freds do it? How did they know a woman was pregnant even if she hid for her entire nine months? How did they overpower everyone without weapons or threats? How did they take our children—the one thing everyone would have joined together to fight for?"

He seemed to be gazing off into the distance. Then he

turned his head back toward me. I knew he couldn't see. But it still felt like we had a connection, his brown eyes on my green ones.

We were thinking the same thing.

"The Freds had to have been from outer space too," he finished.

CHAPTER
FORTY

"**That's all** I know," my father said. "Now get back inside. Quick. Before someone sees you."

Numbly, I squeezed past the splintered door once more and back into the house. My mind was reeling; my world was reeling.

So everything the Freds told us was a lie? I wondered. *They fooled us, they tricked us, they . . .*

My mother placed a bundle in my arms.

"You have to go," she said. "Now."

Her voice was strict—cruel, even—but I could hear the throbbing pain and sorrow buried in her words. Had that pain been hidden in everything she ever said to me? And I never fully understood until I found out that the Freds had deep secrets too?

"I—Bobo and I need to say good-bye to our father," I said dazedly. "I didn't say good-bye just now. I—"

"He'll understand!" she insisted. Her green eyes, so like

mine, glinted with pain in her ruined face. "He wants you to be safe. We can't let anyone else find you here. And there's already been such a commotion. . . ."

Dimly I realized that lots of people had to have heard the Enforcer shooting our door off its hinges, then his gun going off when my parents and Drusa attacked him. Somewhere nearby a dog howled. More Enforcers would come soon. They'd follow the trail of whining and barking and howling dogs. They'd find the splintered door, the tracks left in the dirt road where my father had dragged the Enforcer away.

"It's not safe for you to stay here either!" I protested.

"It's not safe for you and Bobo and Cana if we don't stay here, hiding the evidence," she retorted. "And lying about where you've gone. Look."

She took me by the shoulders and turned me to face Bobo and Cana, who were waiting beside Drusa. Their eyes were wide, watching me. Bobo had his shoes on now; he and Cana both had small bundles tied to their backs.

They were ready to go. If anything happened to them before we left, it would be my fault.

Of course, it would also be my fault if anything happened to them after we left.

"We'll go," I said. "Good-bye, and . . ."

I hugged my mother and she whispered, "Take care of Bobo. Take care of yourself."

It was hard to let go, even of my real mother, who I'd thought hated me. Maybe my father had avoided saying good-bye on purpose.

There was nothing left to say. There was everything left to say. Even all the time in the world wouldn't be enough.

"Go now," Drusa urged, shoving Cana and Bobo toward me. "You'll have to sneak out the back window, over to the creek, then toward the mountains. . . . Oh, be careful. . . ."

The two women propelled me out of the house, into the darkness of the backyard. Then they handed Bobo and Cana out to me over a windowsill. For the first few steps I took away from our house, away from our yard, I could still feel their hands on my shoulder, could still hear their voices in my ear: Go. . . . Be careful. . . . I could still hear my father's voice saying, The Freds had to have been from outer space too.

But then, as Bobo and Cana and I crept into an alley-way, chickens squawked at our passing and I realized I had to snap out of this numb daze. I couldn't think about the Freds or the Enforcer's beetle face right now. I had to think about avoiding danger—about watching for Enforcers on patrol and for dark-eyed people who hated green-eyed people like me. (What color were Cana's eyes? I'd have to remember to look once we reached any type of light—knowing could mean the difference between life and death.)

"How far do we have to walk?" Bobo asked in his normal, everyday loud voice.

I had to keep Bobo and Cana quiet without terrifying them beyond belief.

"It's a long way," I whispered back to Bobo. "But it will be more fun if we play a game. How about . . . the quiet game? If you can tiptoe in absolute silence between here and the creek, I'll carry your bundles along with mine after that."

He fell for it. I wasn't sure if Cana fell for it too or if she understood enough to be quiet anyhow. But both of them started taking exaggerated steps, placing their feet down without so much as snapping a twig or rustling a leaf.

I was the one who made the first noise: letting out a quiet sigh of relief when I saw the first glint of the creek through the trees ahead. It would be safer along the water, away from people. We turned toward the ruins Edwy and I had visited only the night before, and that gave me more I had to avoid thinking about: Edwy, the wasteland I'd seen by moonlight, the children who had died there in the war.

And it's still not safe to think about the Freds, or the Enforcer's beetle face, or what my mother and Drusa are doing to hide the splintered door or to brush over the place in the dirt where my father dragged the Enforcer's body. . . .

Bobo and Cana stayed quiet as we walked along the creek, even once we reached the darkness of the ruins. Maybe they'd forgotten that the silent game could end. Maybe they were just as scared and numb as I was. But I felt better with every step that took us farther from the lights of the town, farther from that nightmare place of Enforcers and guns and violence. Could I dare to hope that we really would escape?

We were at the outer edge of the ruins when Cana tugged on my hand.

"Is that a firefly following us?" she whispered.

"What?" I whispered back. "Fireflies don't follow people."

I could have told her I hadn't seen a single firefly in our hometown. Fireflies belonged back in Fredtown, back with those carefree summer nights when our Fred-parents let us stay up late to run across dewy lawns, chasing the fireflies' glow.

Cana tugged on my hand again and pointed.

"That one is," she said.

I turned just in time to see a dot of light behind us stop moving. It hovered in the air as if suspended, waiting for us to make the next move.

Should I cry *Run!* to Bobo and Cana? Or *Hide!*?

During the moment I hesitated, Bobo took a step back.

"Hello, Mr. Firefly," he called. "Can't you come closer so we can see you better?"

No! I wanted to scream. *Bobo, you're putting us in danger!*

But before I could grab his hand and take off running,

the glow of light sped closer. And grew. And grew. In less than a second, I could see that it wasn't just a pinpoint of light. It was a person.

But it wasn't an Enforcer. Or a murderous attacker bent on destroying all green-eyed people or all dark-eyed people.

It was someone I knew.

A Fred.

CHAPTER
FORTY-ONE

"Mrs. Osemwe?" Cana asked. For it did indeed seem to be the principal of our school from back in Fredtown, moving toward us. The same woman who had passed out hugs the day we left.

"I missed you!" Bobo squealed, letting go of my hand and launching himself toward her glow.

But right at the point where he started to wrap his arms around her waist in a gigantic hug, his arms went right through her middle. He fell through her legs, landing on the ground.

"Bobo, that's only the *image* of Mrs. Osemwe," Cana called, in the same patient tone that she would have used to explain the alphabet. "Like you might see on TV. Or in a movie projected on a sheet."

Once again, Cana had figured out something ahead of me.

"Oh," Bobo said. "Why didn't you tell me that before I scraped my knee?"

I knew Bobo expected sympathy and a hand up, and maybe even a piece of candy to take his mind off his knee. But I didn't have time for that.

"Mrs. Osemwe, you've got to stop glowing," I said in a tone I never would have used with a grown-up back in Fredtown. "You're going to call attention to us. That's"—it had to be said, even if Bobo and Cana were listening—"that's putting us in danger. It's not safe."

"I only glow forward, not behind," Mrs. Osemwe said, her voice tinny and distant, as if it came from a million kilometers away. "I am only darkness behind. I am hiding you."

"It's true—I can't see her anymore from here," Bobo said. He rolled back toward me and Cana. Now it looked like he was playing a game that involved crawling around Mrs. Osemwe's ankles. "Now I can." He popped up his head behind Mrs. Osemwe again. "Now I can't." He giggled. "This is fun."

"Bobo, shh!" I snapped. "Someone will hear! Mrs. Osemwe—"

"I put up a sound barrier around us too," Mrs. Osemwe said. "Don't worry."

Her voice still seemed distant, and I could hear a falseness in it that I'd never noticed back in Fredtown. Was it because this was only her image, not really her? Was it because she spoke in an accent different from that of my real parents and I'd gotten used to them in the past few days?

Or was it because she was an alien and her real mouth and real face weren't designed for human speech?

I should have been relieved to see Mrs. Osemwe's image, to have any link to the comfort and safety of Freds and Fredtown.

But the sight of her calm, smooth, peaceful face just made me mad.

I was running for my life. I was terrified that I might make some mistake that could lead to Bobo's and Cana's deaths. And my own. I'd learned that my real hometown was full of hatred and pain. I'd hit and kicked and punched—I'd *fought*—at a moment when I didn't know what else I could possibly have done.

I didn't understand peace anymore.

"Mrs. Osemwe, I didn't think Freds were allowed to come home with us," I said, and I sounded just as bitter and angry as Edwy ever did back in Fredtown.

"We weren't," she said. "We aren't. The intergalactic court ruled against all our appeals."

"But you can send an image," I said. "Why didn't you send an image of every one of our Fred-parents with us, right from the start? Why didn't you do that to . . ."

Guide us, I thought. *Protect us. Keep us from making the kind of mistakes I made.*

Mrs. Osemwe frowned. I had never seen a Fred frown before.

"Even sending an image is . . . bending the rules," she said. "Exploiting a loophole."

"Bending rules is wrong," Cana said, as primly as if we were sitting in the Fredtown school. "Almost as bad as breaking them."

"But we had to do something," Mrs. Osemwe said. "You're children. We couldn't let you . . . the three of you . . ." She glanced toward Cana and Bobo, still sprawled on the ground by her ankles, and stopped. Had she been about to say "suffer"? "fail"? "die"? Would she have finished her sentence if I had been the only one standing before her?

"I came to take you back to Fredtown," she finished.

I expected Bobo and Cana to jump up and down and cheer. I would have expected my own heart to leap with joy. I'd wanted to return to Fredtown ever since I'd left it.

But neither Bobo nor Cana nor I moved.

"Fredtown isn't even on Earth, is it?" I finally asked.

Mrs. Osemwe looked toward Cana and Bobo.

"No," she admitted. She flicked her gaze back to me and seemed to be trying to smile. "So, see, Rosi, you did get to be an astronaut traveling through space as you always dreamed. You just . . . didn't know it."

If she expected me to clap gleefully and shout, *Hurray!*

That's so cool! like I would have when I was little, she didn't know anything about me.

"But how . . . ?" I said. "Why . . . ?"

"We made you think it was just a plane ride back to your parents, because that was more appropriate for the humans you were rejoining," she said. "But really there were wormholes, quantum travel, illusions. We Freds have technology that would have allowed us to zap you back here in no time flat, but the intergalactic court ruled that you needed more of a transition than that. More of a sense of distance."

So that we didn't think we could just run away, back to Fredtown? I wondered.

"Fredtown *is* on a planet in another galaxy," Mrs. Osemwe continued. "We couldn't take you back there now without letting you see that."

"Another galaxy," Cana repeated numbly. "Another planet."

"Ooh," Bobo said. "You're another space person. Like the beetle man. Do you have a beetle face too? Can I see it?"

Mrs. Osemwe hesitated.

"My true face isn't a beetle's," she said. "We Freds are a different species from the Enforcers. From a different planet. A different part of the universe. With entirely different outlooks and goals."

But she touched her chin and her human face parted,

revealing soft mint-green fur below. It was hard to make out eyes and a nose and a mouth, exactly—was it possible that Mrs. Osemwe had *three* noses and *six* eyes? But the gentle kindness that had always shown through her human features was just as clearly written in her alien expression.

"Cool," Bobo said. "That's the kind of face I'd want, if I had a second one."

"Why didn't you let us see that from the start in Fredtown?" I asked. "We wouldn't have been afraid. You taught us never to be afraid of anyone based on appearances. You taught us not even to care about appearances. But *you* cared. You cared enough to hide your real faces from all of us."

"You needed *human* role models to help you grow up properly," Mrs. Osemwe said. She touched her chin again, and her familiar human face reappeared. "Or at least the illusion of those role models. All our studies—all our past interactions with other violent species—showed that you needed to think there were peaceable adults of your own kind for you to emulate."

"So why didn't you just send us somewhere else on Earth?" I asked. I cast my eyes toward Bobo and Cana, but I *had* to ask the rest of my question. Even if they heard it. "Why didn't you send us somewhere on Earth where no one had ever killed anyone over what kind of eyes they had?"

"Because in other places on Earth, people were fighting

too," Mrs. Osemwe said bitterly, in a tone that was entirely wrong, coming from her gentle face. "They were fighting over skin color or shoes or land or oil or olive trees or church buildings. Don't you understand? When we took away the children of your hometown to raise you in a peaceful fashion, we took away all the other human babies too. For twelve years, we took away every infant born on Earth."

CHAPTER FORTY-TWO

I don't know what Cana and Bobo understood of Mrs. Osemwe's words, but I couldn't seem to fit them into my brain.

"Then—there isn't anywhere safe for us to go on Earth?" I asked. "Anywhere where people will treat us like . . ."

Like worthy human beings, I almost said. When I guess what I really meant was, *Like Freds.*

"There are *safer* places," Mrs. Osemwe said sadly. "But nowhere fully safe. That's why you have to come back to Fredtown."

Why did I pick that moment to be like Edwy—to hate being told what to do? Why, when she was saying I had to do what I'd wanted all along?

Mrs. Osemwe must have misinterpreted the confusion in my eyes, because she added, "Fredtown number one, I mean. There are actually thousands of Fredtowns we created on one of our surplus planets, all corresponding to an actual town or city here on Earth."

It took me a moment to absorb that. The place I was homesick for—my longed-for Fredtown—wasn't even unique. It was just one of thousands of copies.

"So you took us away and then the Enforcers brought us back and now you and the other Freds . . . you *renegotiated* with all the human parents on Earth," Cana said, pronouncing each syllable of *renegotiated* with more precision than most five-year-olds could handle. Most five-year-olds wouldn't have even known what the word meant. "You got them to let all of us kids go back to our own Fredtown, where we'll be safe."

"No," Mrs. Osemwe said, and even she sounded a little impatient. "We can only take the three of you back. We have to abide by the rules of the intergalactic court."

"You mean, you're afraid of the Enforcers, too," I said, disheartened. "They have control over you just like they do over this town."

"*No,*" Mrs. Osemwe said. Her expression was the closest thing to a scowl that I'd ever seen on any Fred's face. "Under intergalactic rules, no mature civilization has control over any other. We coexist peacefully, although . . ." She shook her head, as if trying to dislodge an unpleasant thought. "All mature, thinking civilizations are represented in the intergalactic court. But let's just say that some species have vastly different opinions about how to deal with immature civilizations that are still mired in violence even as they inch their way out into space, endangering others. . . ."

Like humans, I thought.

It hurt to hear my own species called "immature" and "mired in violence." But wasn't that what I'd seen in my own hometown? Hadn't I myself reacted to violence with more violence?

Did the rest of the universe see human violence as a virus that threatened to infect everyone?

"Enforcers are violent, too," I said defensively. "Enforcers are even worse than humans. Aren't they? Why aren't they punished and sent away?"

I sounded like a little kid tattling, telling the teacher, *Maybe I cheated a little bit, but not as bad as Edwy! He copied down every answer! Punish him, not me!*

Mrs. Osemwe sighed.

"We Freds and the Enforcers stand at opposite ends of . . . mature, civilized thought," she murmured, glancing quickly at Bobo and Cana, then back at me. "The Enforcers think containment is the only way to deal with an immature, violent species. They think you answer force with greater force, to keep violent societies from spilling over into the rest of the universe."

"But how are they allowed to—" *Act like it's fun to shoot people*, I wanted to say. *Call it hunting rabbits. Treat us like we're not even human.*

It was impossible to say any of that to Mrs. Osemwe's kind, caring face. It was too shameful.

"The Enforcers maintain that everything they do is in service to law enforcement," Mrs. Osemwe said in a tightly controlled voice. "They are peaceful in their interactions with other citizens of their own civilizations and, indeed, all mature civilizations."

I didn't have to be Edwy to feel that Mrs. Osemwe was hiding something.

Maybe that she doesn't like the Enforcers, either? I thought. *Maybe she even hates them?*

"Shall we focus on what the Freds have tried to do instead?" Mrs. Osemwe said, sounding almost like her usual cheerful self again. She even smiled. "We Freds lead long lives. That makes us patient. Patient enough to look for good, even in dangerous species. You humans have so much potential, and we had the time to help you develop it. We thought if we managed to raise up an entire generation in peace, if we waited until you were adults before we fully revealed your heritage and gave you the choice of whether to return to Earth, then—"

"We aren't adults yet," Cana said in her whispery little-girl voice. I'd almost forgotten she and Bobo were there. I was too caught up in Mrs. Osemwe's words. "We didn't have a choice, coming here."

Mrs. Osemwe turned her head to the side and peered out into darkness.

"After we got involved, humans stayed peaceful just long enough to win a seat on the intergalactic court as probationary members," she said, and now her voice ached with pain. "They proved particularly persuasive, casting us Freds as the villains. As child-snatchers. Even though we sent food and other supplies to all the adults left behind on Earth, even though we were doing nothing to physically harm anyone . . ."

But you took away their children, I thought. And it was like I was hearing my real parents' voices in my head. My real mother and father could never see the Freds as anything but kidnappers. That was why they despised them so much. That was why they'd hated me talking and acting like a Fred, even as I ached to be back with the Freds. Even as they themselves were trapped in a place where violence still simmered below the surface.

Where just having us kids come home was enough to make it boil over.

"But now you can take us back to Fredtown?" I asked, and I hated how my voice broke, saying that. "Us, but only us? How could that be?"

"Only because you now count as fugitives," Mrs. Osemwe said. "Only because of that loophole. And . . . it's an iffy one.

That's why I'm doing this in secret. We have to leave all the other human children right where they are."

She might as well have added: *Stuck on Earth. In danger.*

I thought about Edwy, wherever he was, and how he and I had promised to watch out for each other. I still owed him that. I thought of all the other children who had come from Fredtown only days ago—like Meki, whose real father yelled at her; like Aili, whose father showed little more concern for her than for the red bow in her hair. I thought about my real parents and Cana's mother, and how they were probably risking their lives right now to make sure that Bobo, Cana, and I got away.

"If we go back to Fredtown—*our* Fredtown, I mean—," I said slowly, "I know we'll be safe. But will we be able to *do* anything? To help anyone left behind on Earth?"

"No," Mrs. Osemwe said. Was it just my imagination, or did she seem to fade a little into the darkness?

I thought of living in Fredtown with just Freds and Bobo and Cana. In some ways, it wouldn't be that different from hiding in the hollowed-out space under my real parents' living room floor. There'd be nothing to do. Nothing *real*. Nothing that mattered. Nothing that justified someone coming from another planet to save my life. Especially not twice.

"We can't go," I said. "I can't."

"What? How can you make that decision?" Mrs. Osemwe asked. "You're in danger."

"Because this is the decision you and the other Freds taught me to make," I said. I swallowed hard. *"The purpose of human life is to serve, and to show compassion and the will to help others.* Albert Schweitzer. That's a founding principle of Fredtown. That's what you and the other Freds always told me. And that's why I'm staying on Earth, where I can help my friends and family. Somehow. Someday." I looked down at Cana and at Bobo, who was still sprawled on the ground. It pained me to say what I had to say next. "But maybe, since they're so young, Bobo and Cana should . . ."

"No," Cana said, shaking her head firmly. "The Freds taught *me* to help, too. *Our prime purpose in this life is to help others.* The Dalai Lama."

"I don't know all the principles yet, but I'm not leaving Rosi," Bobo said. "She *needs* me."

"Can't you help us with what we want to do here?" I asked Mrs. Osemwe.

"No," she said sadly. "No, no . . ."

And then she was gone.

CHAPTER
FORTY-THREE

I didn't feel like an orphan after all.

That was yet another surprise.

As Mrs. Osemwe's image faded away and Bobo, Cana, and I were left in the darkness again, I expected to feel bereft. Turning down Mrs. Osemwe's offer probably meant I would never see my Fred-parents again. Maybe it meant I would never be safe again.

But I could feel everything my Fred-parents had ever taught me embedded inside me. What I'd witnessed and experienced and learned in my hometown made me see them differently. But they were still a part of me, and always would be. And I still loved my Fred-parents, even if I couldn't go back to them.

Now that I understood my real parents a little better, I could feel their love for me too. I was even thinking of them as "*my* parents," not "*the*." I wasn't sure when that had started.

They were confusing people—they had awful secrets. But they belonged to me.

Was it because I understood fighting back now? Was it because I knew the story behind their scars?

Or was it because I finally understood that they had loved me all along, even when I was on another planet? And that they were willing to put their own lives in danger to keep me safe?

"Shouldn't we keep walking?" Cana asked anxiously.

"Yes," I said. "Come on."

Bobo sprang up from the ground, and the three of us turned away from our hometown, away from the wasteland where children had been killed. It was awful to still be in this place, to still be in danger. To still be on a planet where all children—and maybe even all people—were in danger. But it would have been worse to leave it without even trying to help. And, stepping forward, we were at least entering new territory, places I hadn't seen the night before with Edwy. In the moonlight, I could just barely make out the contour of a mountain ahead of us.

When we got to that mountain, maybe we would find Edwy, safe and sound. Or maybe we would have to find a way to save him, along with everyone else.

"'Membrance,'" Bobo told Cana. "Rosi says that's what that mountain is called."

"Remembrance," I corrected him. "It's, like, a memory. Remembering the past. But I think we should call it something different now."

"What?" Cana said.

"Better Times Ahead, maybe?" I said. "Because that's what we're going to find there."

I hoped that I was telling the truth.